MESSENGER

THE SHIFTER WAR BOOK ONE

K K NESS

ACKNOWLEDGMENTS

We acknowledge the Bindal and Wulgurukaba people upon whose Country this book was written.

1

———

Danil hunkered down beside the meltwater stream as it cut a new path over burnt soil. Cold bit into his skin as he submerged his pan of rocks and dirt into the water and shook. He tilted the pan towards the afternoon sun, hoping for the telltale iridescent flash to indicate he'd found a vein of magic-laden crystal.

Nothing.

Danil's shoulders sank as he upended the gritty dirt. If his luck didn't turn soon, he'd have nothing to placate the mage back home at Farin. The skin on his back tightened at the thought.

Wiping a damp sleeve across his forehead, Danil shoveled another load of charred soil. The meltwater stream disappeared down into an abandoned mineshaft only a few feet away, making a low rushing sound as it filled the tunnels. Danil kept a trained ear out for the warning crack and rumble of the earth giving way. The deadland mines had taken many careless folk over the centuries, and the last weeks of winter always proved the most perilous.

But mineshafts were among the lesser threats of the

deadlands. A befouled magic shaped the great expanse of rock separating the kingdoms of Roldaer and Amas. Danil grew up on tales of a formerly lush and verdant forest turned to blackened waste by a tremendous explosion that ended the Great War three centuries ago. Nothing grew save for groves of poisonous fungi, and no animal dared make its home in the nooks and crevices. Only a handful of Roldaerians like Danil made the gamble of wandering the deadlands in search of old battlefield relics, smoky quartz and the very rare mage-crystals.

The greatest danger, however, was the Amasian shapeshifters.

By habit, Danil cast a wary glance across the barren expanse to the green line of forest and mountains a half day's walk to the west. The shapeshifters of Amas no doubt observed him from the shadowed trees. Even the mackerel-striped clouds scudding overhead likely hid a hawk shifter or two. Tall and powerful creatures, the Amasians allowed scavenging in the deadlands, so long as no one strayed too close to their border or attempted to walk away with mage-crystals.

One shifter in particular took pleasure in ambushing Danil to examine his daily findings.

A problem at a time, Danil reminded himself, sloshing icy water about the pan. Magus Ronan would use his firewhip if Danil didn't miraculously find a mage-crystal to appease him.

Danil had perhaps an hour before there was no choice but to make the dangerous trek back to Farin empty-handed. Tipping out the sludge, he headed for a new dig site beside a boulder that sat partially submerged in the meltwater. Water eddied in a lazy circle at its base. Danil shoveled out a small load and vigorously shook the pan.

A flash of orange amidst the blackened mud caught his eye. Danil fished out a pebble no larger than his thumbnail. A thin, iridescent vein glittered up at him, turning purple then emerald before changing to a deep blue. Pleasant warmth spread across Danil's palm.

Finally!

Glancing carefully across to the forested border of Amas, Danil tucked the pebble into the pouch at his hip and emptied out the remains of his pan. If he was lucky, he'd be halfway across the deadlands before the Amasian shapeshifters sensed what he'd found. He quickly strapped the pan to the outside of his pack before storing away his shovel.

A shower of rocks clattered down the nearby embankment. Danil froze, studying the mound of shale. He knew better than to hope that an animal had dislodged the rocks. Cursing softly under his breath, he slowly rose to his feet and turned.

A massive red wolf stood in his path.

Danil cursed a little louder.

The powerful creature stood as tall as Danil's chest—far too tall to be anything but an Amasian shapeshifter. Its coat was handsome red with a pale ruff and white socks. Bright green eyes twinkled merrily as the wolf stepped up onto a small outcrop. It posed in the sun, coat gleaming and broad tail waving in the air like a streamer.

Hafryn...

The air about the wolf shimmered, and from one heartbeat to the next the wolf transformed into a man—a very naked and unabashed man with a handsomely freckled face and red hair that brushed over broad shoulders.

The man extended his arms above his head, spine popping loudly. "That got it," he said, twisting with relish.

"Damned deadlands is murder on my Trueform." He made a show of stretching out the various kinks in his body.

Danil eyed him suspiciously, taking slow steps toward the meltwater stream.

"Where are you off to?" Hafryn said as he eventually lowered his arms. "Anyone would think you're not glad to see me."

That wasn't much of a stretch. Out of all of the shifters he'd come across, Hafryn was the most tenacious, and had an unerring ability to show up exactly when Danil didn't want him to.

Danil noticed the wolf running an assessing gaze over the pack held in his fist. "You're here to steal from me again," he said with a sigh.

Hafryn hopped down from the rock with easy grace. "Well, you always find the prettiest things, Danil."

Danil couldn't help but gape. "Last week you stole my cloak."

Hafryn's mouth tilted upwards. "That wasn't my finest moment," he admitted. "But every other human is so *boring*. Have you met the folk from Scara?" He shuddered.

Scara was the only other village that rode the edge of the deadlands. Danil hadn't spoken to anyone there in many summers but knew they were a terse lot.

"Well, I've got nothing of interest today, either," Danil said, resisting the urge to fold his arms. "Just more of those arrowheads up by the scree fields."

Hafryn scrunched his nose. "Hardly worth the risk, wouldn't you say?"

Danil shrugged. "I figure I can sell them to a soldier." There was always folk among the magi's personal guard with a liking for old battlefield relics.

"I suppose. Doesn't explain why you're out here so late,

though," Hafryn said, taking a quick glance at the snow-capped mountains already turning pink by the setting sun. "Normally you know better. Does it have anything to do with the mage who arrived last week?"

Danil squinted. The shifters truly missed nothing.

The wolf grinned. "Lord Runtface, am I right?"

"Magus Ronan," Danil corrected. He cast an uneasy glance toward the village. Most magi despised their stint in Farin, and were quick to assuage their wrath on the villagers. Magus Ronan was no exception, as the old scars on Danil's back attested.

Only the Great War treaty made Farin worthy of a mage's visit. After the drubbing Roldaer received at the hands of Amas three centuries ago, the treaty ensured both kingdoms stayed firmly on their respective side of the deadlands. The task of guaranteeing no Roldaerian broke the treaty and entered Amas was left to the magi—who resoundingly found the duty beneath them.

"Lord Runtface been using that whip of his yet?" Hafryn asked.

"Not yet," Danil managed, skin turning cold at the thought of the spell-infused weapon.

"Then he needn't find out about that crystal in your pouch," Hafryn said easily.

Danil stilled but knew his face betrayed him.

"I can sense it from here, Danil," the wolf said. He motioned with his hand. "Give it over."

Taking a step back, Danil glanced nervously at the meltwater. It flowed too fast for safe passage, but the wolf was already drawing closer. "Hafryn—"

"You know the deal. For all that you found the crystal here, it tumbled down from the mountains of Amas," Hafryn said. He stepped over a large piece of slate. "It belongs to Amas, not the magi."

But without the mage-crystal, Magus Ronan's firewhip was going to burn Danil's flesh that very night.

He took another step back, feeling water lap at the edge of his boots. "It's not yours to take, Hafryn."

"It really is."

Without thinking, Danil wrenched loose the shovel from his pack and swung it blindly. "Stay back. I mean it!"

The wolf shifter stopped in astonishment. "You can't possibly be serious."

Danil swung the shovel back and forth in warning. "Back!"

Hafryn stayed just beyond reach, hands splayed wide. "You're really going to fight me on this?"

Baring his teeth, Danil said, "You give me no choice." He swung the shovel again, missing the wolf by more than a foot. "Get *back!*"

A new, hungry light filled Hafryn's eyes. "Oh, Danil," he murmured. "Say the word and I'll keep you forever."

Danil scowled. "I'm not kidding, Hafryn."

"I know. That's what makes you so precious."

Lightning-quick, Hafryn ducked under the shovel and smacked it away with startling force. It skittered across the pebbles to the stream's edge. Before Danil could flinch, the wolf yanked the pouch on his hip. It broke loose with a snap.

"Ha!" Hafryn said, bounding away like a pup with a stick.

"Hey!" Danil lunged after him, growling as Hafryn danced across the stones, the pouch held high. "Give it back!" He leapt, too short to reach.

Hafryn grinned, putting his free hand on Danil's chest to hold him off. "Now, now, don't get mad."

Danil glared furiously, feeling his cheeks flush as he jumped again for the pouch. "Gods damn it, Hafryn!"

The wolf shifter grinned down at him. "I've never seen you this angry. It's rather fetching—Oof!"

Danil punched him squarely in the gut. Hafryn doubled over, wheezing. Snatching the pouch from slackened fingers, Danil bolted up the alluvial bank. A small wave of stones cascaded down behind him. He clambered over a scorched boulder and dashed for the scree field.

A heavy weight slammed into his back. Danil crashed hard into jagged rocks, grazing his chin and elbows. Large hands attempted to prize the pouch from his grip, but Danil desperately curled around it.

Hafryn easily rolled Danil onto his back before sitting down on his thighs. Danil wriggled frantically, but the shifter grabbed his wrist and squeezed until the pain made Danil lose his grip on the pouch.

"Stop, Hafryn, that hurts!"

The wolf scooped up the pouch and shook out the small pebble. Held up to the afternoon light, the magic-laden vein flashed pink then yellow.

"Lovely," the shifter murmured. He glanced down at Danil. "Not as lovely as you, of course. I'm sorry I hurt your face."

Danil whacked him in the chest. "Get off me."

Hafryn merely sat back, looking comfortable. "I've wondered what it would take to get you under me, Danil."

Danil set his jaw mutinously. "Not this. Get *off*."

The wolf gave an amused huff. "Alright, fine, you prude." He rose to his feet. "You should get over that shyness, you know. You're too delightful to be uptight."

"I'll take it under advisement," he muttered sourly.

Refusing to look at the shifter's nether regions just

inches from his face, Danil eased himself up into sitting position, his back one long bruise. Frustration formed a lump in his throat—he'd have to stay in the deadlands for the night to avoid Magus Ronan's fury.

Then something cold and circular landed in his lap. Danil glanced down to see an ancient battlefield coin, its Roldaerian phoenix crest worn down in parts to bare gold. He stared at it in confusion. It was enough to feed everyone in Farin for a month.

"Give it to Lord Runtface."

Danil blinked up at Hafryn.

"It'll appease him, won't it?" the wolf pressed.

It wasn't a mage-crystal, but it just might suit the mage's greed. Still, Danil glowered at Hafryn's nakedness. "I don't even want to know where you pulled it from," he said dourly.

"I can show you, if you like," Hafryn said, then laughingly raised his hands when Danil's expression darkened. "Another time."

Danil tucked the coin into his pocket, feeling strangely uncomfortable. "Thank you," he murmured. "Even if you did just rob me."

"The pleasure is all mine."

Danil's eyes narrowed.

With a laugh, the wolf scruffed Danil's hair. "I do treasure our time together, Danil. Truly."

He popped the crystal in his mouth and winked. A moment later, Hafryn transformed into his red timber wolf Trueform. He towered over Danil sitting amid the rocks, yet Danil didn't flinch. Green eyes approving, the wolf bolted across the rocks, tail waving like a banner.

Moments later, Hafryn was gone.

2

D anil limped his way past scraggly tufts of grass at the outskirts of Farin. Night cast long shadows on the squat huts and dirty patches of snow lining the muddy road. Everything hurt, and with deadland grit imbedded in the skin of his knees and elbows, Danil knew he needed doctoring.

Stupid, thieving shifter, he thought, not for the first time. He'd have to barter with Vellum for healing salves come morning. If he dared knock on her door tonight, she'd charge him double.

Cursing Hafryn again under his breath, Danil trudged past the outermost huts. Firelight showed between the cracks in the window shutters. It was surprisingly quiet, with even old Hannah's dog not bothering to emerge from behind the pigpen to accost him. At least his own hut was just a short distance away, its thatched roof limned with moonlight. He yearned for his sleeping pallet and a moment to absorb the happenings of the day.

The scuff of boots on stone made him turn in time to see

four strangers step out from the shadows. Two moved quickly to his flank with swords drawn, while another pointed his spear at Danil's throat.

He slowly raised his hands.

"Who the hell are you?" the leader asked. She wore a silver pin on her pale tabard that marked her as a commander of a mage's personal guard. Her dark hair was shaved at the sides in the manner of folk from the royal city of Anteran.

Glancing about, Danil noted that each stranger wore a pale blue tabard with the six-starred symbol of the magi, combined with an insignia of a charging battle horse. It wasn't the insignia worn by Magus Ronan's soldiers, and none of the strangers looked familiar.

"Answer me!" the commander snarled. The soldier beside her tightened his grip on the spear.

Danil raised his hands higher, speaking his name in a rush. "That's my hut over there," he added, pointing. They were close enough to see the peeling paint on his door.

The woman's mouth thinned. "What were you doing coming out of the deadlands?"

"Searching for deadland relics. See?" Danil moved slightly to display the pan strapped to the outside of his pack. "I would have been back by sundown, but I...fell."

"Can't be very good for a deadland rat, then, can you?" the commander sneered.

The two soldiers behind Danil crowded in close.

"I'm the only one in Farin." Danil tried a weak smile. Most deadland scavengers came from Scara, a day's ride south where the distance between Roldaer and Amas was the greatest. The pickings were poor, but at least running afoul of shifters was rare.

"I know my way about these parts," Danil continued. "But the scree fields were disturbed over winter and so—"

"Your waffle doesn't interest me, rat," the commander said. "Who else is still out in the deadlands?"

Danil blinked. "No one."

"Are you certain?" the commander pressed.

Danil nodded. He'd not even seen folk from Scara in the far distance.

"Very well, then."

At her signal, one of the soldiers yanked the pack off Danil's shoulders and handed it over. The commander opened the top flap and upended the contents into the mud. Her lip curled when his shovel, water flagon and the two arrowheads spilled out.

"Not much of a haul, rat," she said with a sneer. "Search him."

The two soldiers pinioned his arms while their companion patted him down. Danil held his breath as the soldier fished out the coin from his pocket and handed it to the commander.

"What are you doing with this?" she asked, turning it about so that the gold caught in the torchlight.

"It's for Magus Ronan," Danil said.

One of the soldiers gripping his arms snorted. "Sure it is."

Danil glanced at him in surprise.

"All deadland wealth belongs to the magi," the commander said. "Need I explain that stealing from our illustrious mages is a capital offence?"

"No, of course not," Danil said quickly.

The commander shared a dark grin with her companions. "And yet you attempted to hide this."

Danil gaped as the grip on his arms turned bruising. "It was in my pocket. I didn't hide anything!"

"Save your excuses for the magi," she snarled.

"But—"

Without warning, she punched him in the belly. Danil doubled over, gasping for breath as the commander struck him again.

A flurry of blows rained down from every direction, knocking him into the mud. Someone kicked him in the back. His vision whitened. He rolled, desperate to get to his feet only to be pummeled once again.

"What's going on here?"

The beating abruptly stopped. Danil lay in the mud, gasping. His ribs were on fire, his mouth full of blood. Blinking spots from his eyes, he craned his neck to see Magus Ronan astride a powerful bay mare. Blonde hair was pulled back in a severe braid, the mage's mouth surly as he yanked viciously on the reins of his horse.

"Get him up."

Danil's vision darkened at the edges as he was roughly hauled to his feet. The two soldiers dragged him to where Magus Ronan sat on his horse.

Recognition flared in the mage's pale eyes. "Well, well. If it isn't the town scavenger," Ronan said. He sat back in the saddle with a smirk, his cloak unfurling to reveal the firewhip coiled at his side. "And yet again you return without a mage-crystal."

Danil swallowed thickly. "Shifter took it," he gasped out.

"Is that so?"

The mage's firewhip flickered red, indicating that it had recently tasted blood but remained hungry.

Danil licked his split lip, knowing no answer could save him.

"Commander Voss," Ronan purred.

"My lord." The commander saluted crisply.

"You reported that all of the villagers had been dealt with."

Danil stared dazedly at the mage. What did he mean by 'dealt with'?

"My lord, this one must have left the village before dawn—"

The mage raised a gloved hand. "Your excuses weary me, commander."

She squared back her shoulders and bowed. "Yes, my lord." She handed Magus Ronan the coin. "He came bearing this."

Ronan gave the coin a cursory look before tucking it into his pouch. "Consider yourself on report, Commander Voss," he said. "This level of incompetence is unacceptable."

The commander saluted again, her expression grim.

"Take him to Lady Brianna."

The commander quickly signaled the two guards. They bodily hauled Danil past Ronan and down the street toward the two-story inn. A series of lanterns out the front revealed a dozen soldiers standing at attention outside. All bore the battle horse insignia on pale blue tabards.

Strangely, Danil didn't see a single villager so much as peek out through the shutters of the huts as he was escorted past.

Where is everyone? Danil wondered as the soldiers dragged him up the three stone steps into the inn.

A wall of cold met him as the door opened to the aleroom. His captors threw Danil across the wooden floor where he fetched up against the legs of a chair. A boot pressed squarely in his back, forcing him facedown onto the floor.

Across the room, the hearth roared at full strength but the air remained stagnant and chill. Ice lined the windows and corners of the aleroom. Danil's breath plumed in the unnatural cold.

Cutlery clinked as someone set aside their evening meal. Danil saw the edge of a fur-lined coat and finely-tooled leather boots.

"My lady, forgive our interruption," Commander Voss said with a deep bow.

"Have we a straggler, commander?" a woman asked. Her voice was mild and finely cultured, more suited to the royal courts of King Liam than an inn at the furthest edge of the kingdom.

"A deadland thief, Magus Brianna," the commander said.

Danil opened his mouth to protest but the boot in his shoulder pressed him down hard.

The woman, Magus Brianna, leaned back in her chair. The scent of roast venison with vegetables and gravy hung thick in the air.

"Let me see."

A hand grabbed a fistful of Danil's hair and forced his head up.

Danil's neck creaked warningly, his eyes watering from the pain. His vision cleared to see a middle-aged woman with a streak of white in her black hair. Pale blue eyes studied him from a delicate, heart-shaped face. She lounged back in her chair and wiped daintily at her mouth with a napkin. At her elbow was a battered, leather bound tome. Strangely, a thick layer of ice coated it. Mist hovered about the book like greedy fingers.

Danil glanced about desperately. A soldier wearing a

pale blue tabard stood behind the bar looking bored, while another stood by the frost-rimed front window. The door leading to the kitchen remained closed. Now that he concentrated, Danil noticed a strange silence when normally the inn rang with the familiar clatter of the cook and her underlings going about their work.

"I was under the impression no one in Farin could survive the deadlands," Magus Brianna said, looking at the commander.

Commander Voss tensed. "I was mistaken, my lady."

"Indeed." The mage turned her cool gaze on Danil. "You look rather young to walk the deadlands with any real familiarity. Does the commander speak true?"

Danil swallowed with an effort. "I'm not a thief, my lady," he muttered, wincing as the grip on his hair tightened. "The innkeeper can vouch for me."

"I'm sure," Magus Brianna said, mouth tilting upwards. "Do you actually walk the deadlands, or merely scavenge the surface?"

It was an odd question. "I know the tunnels, my lady," he hedged.

"Excellent." The mage tapped her fingers on the table, contemplative, before waving her hand. "Let him up, commander. We should not treat our own countryman so harshly."

At her command, the soldiers released Danil and stepped back. Startled, he warily rose to his feet.

Magus Brianna pointed to a chair at her table. "Sit." At his hesitation, she added, "Please."

He walked across and gingerly eased himself down, wincing as bruised muscles protested. The air felt colder still. He glanced cautiously at the ice-bound book—peculiar symbols on the leather writhed across the leather. Danil's skin crawled.

The mage reached across and took his hand in both of hers. "What is your name, my dear?"

Danil glanced uneasily at the soldier behind the bar. The man's posture was relaxed, but his hand rested on his belt close to his sword. "Danil."

She smiled. "A strong Roldaerian name," she said approvingly. "Are you badly hurt, Danil?"

"I—no, my lady."

"Excellent. I shall be sure to have my physician look you over nonetheless." She gave him a smile that didn't reach her eyes.

Danil glanced again at the soldiers spread about the aleroom. "Forgive me, my lady, but where is everyone?"

"Your fellow villagers, you mean?" Magus Brianna shrugged delicately. "I'm afraid they've been evacuated."

Danil mouthed the word, not sure he'd heard right.

"It is for their safety, of course," Brianna continued. "War is brewing and we cannot have our good people in harm's way."

Danil frowned at her. "I-I don't understand."

"Nor would I expect you to," she said. "These are delicate matters. Amas has robbed us for too long."

Perhaps he'd been struck harder than he thought. "We're at war with Amas?"

She gave a tittering laugh. "Dear boy, we have always been at war with those animals!"

Danil bit the inside of his cheek. Living on the edge of the Roldaerian kingdom granted him a certain insight on the Great War treaty. For all his larceny and trickery, Hafryn never treated him like an enemy.

His cheeks warmed at the traitorous thought.

Magus Brianna looked him over. "I must say, you present me with a quandary, Danil. Knowledge of the deadlands is most needed at present, but in times of war, Commander Voss here has the power to rule on a Roldaerian's crimes. If she judges you a thief, then so you are."

The commander's face showed no emotion.

"Of course, your aid in guiding us into the deadlands has the power to change the commander's mind. Isn't that so, Commander Voss?"

"Yes, my lady."

Magus Brianna smiled. "There, you see? In return for your service, you'll be treated most fair, and you'll be with your village friends soon enough."

With a sinking feeling, Danil nodded. "I'd be honored to help, my lady."

"Excellent!" She clapped her hands. "There is a place deep in the deadlands that I've a mind to reach. Have you the skill to guide us?"

Danil managed a nod. "I'd find you safe passage." He hesitated. "But there are no mage-crystals of note left in the deadlands, my lady." He knew how desperately the magi needed the mage-crystals to perform their spells.

"We shall have plenty enough crystals when Amas falls, my dear," she said, her pale eyes gleaming.

Danil couldn't even fake a smile at that.

"Of course, you'll have to stay here at the inn for the night," Magus Brianna continued. "I'm sure you understand." Without waiting for his reply, she motioned to the soldiers behind Danil. "Please escort our guide up to his room."

One of the soldiers who had beaten him edged up close.

Danil mustered a bow to Magus Brianna before he was marched up the stairs to the second floor of the inn. The soldier shoved him into a sparse room with just a pallet on the floor and a battered dresser in one corner.

Before he could turn about, the door slammed shut behind him.

The lock clicked into place with finality.

3

Soldiers patrolled through the dark courtyard below Danil's window with regularity, their boots crunching on the graveled path as they passed.

Danil watched through a crack in the shutters. Unable to sleep, he waited for the pair of soldiers to disappear around the corner of the inn. More of Magus Brianna's soldiers had arrived during the night, slipping quietly into Farin without fanfare. From his vantage point overlooking the stables, Danil had watched as they were billeted into the various empty huts about the village.

A heaviness lay over his heart as he glanced about the sparse room. A pitcher sat untouched on the battered dresser, brought in by a soldier hours before. The pallet was a bundle of moth-eaten blankets, the room itself a remnant of a time when folk visited Farin seeking their fortunes on the deadlands.

Danil gingerly touched a bruise on his jaw. He scarcely believed everyone he knew had abandoned Farin. He never thought he'd find himself accused as a thief with no one to vouch for him.

The kitchen door below him creaked open. Danil peered between the shutters to see Magus Brianna as she stepped out into the muddy courtyard. Mist curled about her feet, growing thicker as she turned to wait for a man in heavy furs to close the door and join her. Moonlight served to brighten the man's white braid and the blood-red whip glowing at his side.

Ronan.

Dislike coiling in his gut, Danil pressed his ear against the wall.

"...dealt with," Ronan was saying, pulling his fur coat tightly about him. "General Valas will be here with the remaining contingent tomorrow. We'll make our sortie by week's end."

"Excellent," Magus Brianna said, walking sedately towards the stables. "We must raid the broken citadel of Altonas quickly."

"Attacking the shifter camps first is our best bet," Ronan said, trailing after her.

Magus Brianna made a soft sound of negation. "The journal indicates otherwise."

"I would prefer not to have an enemy at our back," Ronan muttered, hands clasped behind him. "The dragon prince himself is said to be patrolling the borderlands."

"What is a dragon to the might within Altonas?" Brianna replied, voice bright.

"If what lies within the citadel is as useful as you say, sparing the deadland rat serves no purpose."

Danil held his breath, staring through the shutters.

The woman paused and turned to look at her companion. "That is where we disagree, my friend," she said mildly. "Crossing the deadlands cannot be taken lightly."

"You can't expect the rat to know where the entrance is," Ronan argued.

Danil stared hard, heart thundering. Entrance to what? The deadlands were naught but collapsed tunnels and scorched rock.

"I am certain he does, he just doesn't realize it. According to the journal, there are glyphs designed to turn common folk away."

"Which means he'll take us to the wrong place," Ronan growled.

"Young Danil is motivated to keep his skin intact," Brianna countered. "I think you'll be surprised by how useful he'll prove to be. He found that coin, did he not?"

Ronan muttered something under his breath. His fists clenched behind his back. "He can't be trusted. How do you know he's not listening now?" The mage threw a dark look up at the inn.

Danil ducked out of sight. Blood roared in his ears.

Magus Brianna laughed softly. "A sedative was put in his water. Fear not, he won't wake until I will it so."

Danil glanced across the darkened room to the pitcher lying untouched on the dresser. His mouth thinned.

"You should not be so dour, my friend," Magus Brianna continued. "Today is a great day. Your whip's thirst has been slaked, and we are on the cusp of obtaining all we have ever strived for."

Danil risked a glance out the window to see Ronan scowl.

"I get the rat once you're done with him," the man muttered.

"Of course," Brianna said, disappearing into the stables.

Danil felt the strength drain from his bones. He sank to his knees, his breath hollow in his lungs. They were going to kill him. He'd always known the magi to be hard and merciless, but this was something else.

Shaking his head to clear it, Danil forced himself to his feet. He wouldn't sit about and wait to be slaughtered. Treading across to the door, he carefully tested the handle.

Locked.

Danil pressed his ear to the wood, listening. The floorboards at the far end of the corridor creaked under the weight of a guard.

Pushing himself away from the door, Danil looked again at the window. The drop to the ground below was perilous, even without the regular passage of patrolmen. Only a fool would risk breaking bones to escape.

With little other choice, he checked the courtyard for movement before easing open the shutters. He swung his legs over and grabbed hold of the ledge. His boots scraped upon the rough-hewn clay until he found the tiniest of niches.

He eased himself down, fingers gouging into tiny gaps. His muscles quickly set to burning as he blindly searched for another handhold. After a few moments, his legs dangled above the kitchen door. Closing his eyes, Danil dropped onto the paved steps a few feet below.

He hit the ground with jarring force and lay still, breathless.

The crush of gravel underfoot had him flailing blindly for the door handle. Danil threw himself inside, closing the door behind him. He pressed against it, lungs wheezing. No cry of alarm rang from outside. Glancing quickly about the kitchen, he found it devoid of people.

He slid to the floor in relief, listening as the soldiers marched by on the other side of the door.

The kitchen was stripped unusually bare, the worktable

scrubbed clean and the hearth turned cold and dark. But on the cushioned chair beside the hearth sat the ice-trapped book Danil had seen in the aleroom. Mist billowed across the battered cover, while a layer of ice coated the chair and a wide circle of the stone floor around it.

Danil hesitated.

Perhaps this was the journal the two mages spoke of. The frozen floor had an unnatural, silvery sheen that warned of magic. Whatever the book was, the magi didn't want anyone to touch it.

But Danil equally couldn't bear to see his kingdom at war with Amas. He knew better than most what it meant to go up against a shapeshifter, even one who viewed their interactions as play rather than enmity.

And Amas had long upheld the treaty, demanding nothing of Roldaer in the Great War despite resounding victory.

Taking the book might avert a new war.

Against his better judgement, Danil stepped onto the frozen floor. A shock of pain burst up his legs. Gasping, he snatched up the book. For a heart-stopping moment, his fingers turned to ice. Danil stared in horror, unable to move as a rush of whispers filled his ears. Then blood pumped painfully once more. He gritted his teeth, fingers numb, but held tight as the layer of frost melted under his hands.

He glanced nervously toward the door leading to the aleroom. The inn felt remarkably silent, but Danil knew his luck couldn't hold for long.

With a grimace, he tucked the book under his tunic.

Looks like I really am a thief, he thought with a certain level of vindictiveness.

Hurrying back to the kitchen door, he carefully eased it open. The courtyard was quiet. Thanking the gods, he dashed along the shadows to the far side of the stables where a thin alley spilled out between two huts. Snores resonated from one of the huts, while low, unfamiliar voices murmured in the other.

Danil made it to the spindly grass lining the outskirts of Farin. The book dug into his ribs like an accusation as he studied the oily blackness that marked the edge of the deadlands.

He reached the first line of rock as an enraged scream came from the depths of the village.

4
———

The scrape of boots on rock echoed loudly in the quiet, emanating from somewhere to his left.

Danil pressed his back into the shadow of a boulder and counted six of Magus Brianna's soldiers on the far ridge. Their pale tabards shone whitely, no matter that night still hung thick overhead.

He released a slow, shaky breath.

The remaining soldiers had fallen within an hour of the chase, waylaid by the sprawling shale pits a scant mile from Farin. Their cries had rung out across the barren landscape for a whole day.

Now it was nearing midnight on his second night in the deadlands. Exhaustion pulled at him, but Danil clung to the shadows, watching as the remaining six soldiers disappeared over the ridge and down into the gully beyond.

He'd hoped to make for the village of Scara in the south, but tiny pinpricks of flame in the far distance indicated that soldiers likely searched for him there, too.

Danil pushed off the boulder and darted around a collapsed mineshaft, grimacing as quartz pebbles clattered down into the chasm. The book sat like a cold weight against his chest. It had to be the reason the soldiers refused to call off the hunt.

Stupid, stupid, he berated himself.

No one stood against the magi. They were second to King Liam in power, and only nobles of the highest standing dared to speak ill of them. Danil knew there would be no place to hide in Roldaer, and no one willing to risk Magus Brianna's wrath by concealing a thief.

And yet, despite the burden of stealing the book, Danil couldn't quite compel himself to throw it away. He'd deal with the consequences if it meant stopping Roldaer's plunge into war.

With a steadying breath, Danil made for a series of rock formations made into fantastic shapes by centuries of meltwater. The forested borderland of Amas stood another mile away.

He trudged past the first rock formation, careful of the treacherous shale that sent large plates skittering down the slope. Deep crevasses cut into the boulders. Hard experience had taught him how easy it was to become turned about in this region of the deadlands.

He rounded a corner, guided by fresh air whispering between the rocks and the glint of rutilated crystals in the moonlight.

A hand suddenly clamped over his mouth, wrenching him hard against a powerful chest. Danil flailed wildly, arching his back and kicking with raw terror.

"Danil!" a familiar voice hissed in his ear. "Be still!"

He froze, blood pounding in his ears.

Spun about, he stared up into Hafryn's wide eyes. The shifter wore a tunic of mottled blacks and greys, his breeches similarly dyed to blend with the surrounding rocks.

Frowning, the shifter pressed a finger to his lips.

Danil nodded, and the wolf released him fully.

'*Follow me*,' Hafryn mouthed before slipping into a crevasse that cut deep into the rock.

Danil hesitated, glancing eastward where the soldiers had disappeared. Their voices carried in the air, far closer than he would like.

Hoping he wouldn't regret it, he trailed after the shifter.

Hafryn took him on a wandering path through the sculpted outcrops. They emerged on a flattened strip of pebbles and slabbed stone. The mountains closed in around them, funneling them towards the towering trees that marked the edge of Amas.

Danil slowed as Hafryn took long strides towards the imposing elms.

The wolf shifter turned about. "Hurry up, Danil. It's not just soldiers who hunt you."

Danil glanced nervously at the trees.

Hafryn took cautious steps towards him. "Whatever's happened, Danil, you have sanctuary in Amas."

That was quite a claim. Humans weren't welcome in Amas.

The stupidity of his plan pressed down on him.

Hafryn waited, eyes earnest.

Shaking his head, Danil pulled the book out from under his tunic. "I took this." He handed it over.

Startled disbelief showed in Hafryn's eyes as he ran a thumb over a strange symbol on the leather spine. "This is Amasian. A journal we thought lost to—" He stopped, frowning. "How'd you get this?"

"A mage had it," Danil said. "I think it's important."

"It is."

Strangely, the wolf handed the journal back.

"You've carried it this far," Hafryn said. "And I'm sure at great cost." He turned around, beckoning with one hand as he strode for the tree line. "Come, Danil, let's not tarry."

Danil gaped after the shifter, startled by his easy acceptance and welcome. Perhaps it was foolish to give his trust to Hafryn, but he'd made his choice back in Farin.

Taking a quelling breath, Danil followed the wolf between the soaring trees into Amas.

OTHER SHIFTERS WAITED for them amidst a thicket of tree ferns and patches of snow. A massive black bear stood at the edge of a stream, accompanied by a spotted leopard who tilted her nose up to scent the air. A few others in human form watched him silently, hands on swords. One held a crossbow, though thankfully the bolt was currently pointed at the ground.

Danil glanced tensely at Hafryn, but the wolf appeared unconcerned.

The foremost shifter was a man in his early thirties, heavily muscled with black hair held back in a loose tail. He seemed to take up more space than his size demanded. Some nameless instinct warned Danil not to rile him. He remained very still as the man's golden eyes momentarily flickered with flames at their center.

Hafryn bowed. "Dragon Prince Sonnen," he said, and Danil smothered a startled gasp. "This is Danil of Farin."

The dragon shifter, Sonnen, merely looked him over, expression closed. The surrounding shifters were easier to read, with some wary and others curious.

"Why have you crossed into Amas, Danil of Farin?" Sonnen asked, his voice a deep rumble that inexplicably reminded Danil of rolling thunder during the deep of winter.

Danil straightened his spine and took a deep breath.

"I bring a message of war."

5

They took him to a campsite a few miles into Amas. Like Hafryn, most of the shifters recognized the stolen journal, although only Dragon Prince Sonnen dared touch it. Danil watched in amazement as the dragon wove a flaming symbol over the journal that quenched the last remnants of ice with a hiss.

They peppered him with questions as they moved amongst the trees. Danil answered as best he could, trying to recall the smallest detail of what he'd seen and heard in Farin. To his surprise, none of the shifters appeared startled by Magus Brianna's gathering force.

Now at the campsite, an oversized owl watched Danil from a branch high above. Firelight caught along the glossy edge of its feathers. Danil felt the owl's huge eyes on the back of his neck as he picked at the trailbread a man had given him when they first arrived.

Sonnen sat on the opposite side of the campfire, leafing through pages of the journal as Hafryn and another two shifters leaned over his shoulders to read as well.

The camp itself was a revelation. Brightly colored tents

of reds, greens and blues sat amongst the massive trees, each tent large enough to house a dozen folk. A series of symbols were either dyed or etched into the canvas, and showed golden in the firelight. Chimes hung from the branches throughout the camp, tinkling in the breeze.

"Here," a young woman said, abruptly sitting beside Danil. "Hold out your hands."

The woman was in her twenties, dark-skinned with curling black hair pulled back by a band of tooled leather. Dimples showed as she gave him a smile.

Danil blinked and did as she asked.

She turned Danil's hands about, inspecting the fingertips. "It's as I thought," she muttered. "Frostbite." She pulled out a small jar of ink from a satchel at her side, along with a fine paintbrush. "Damned magi and their cursed tricks. I'm going to do a healing, okay?"

"Uh, sure," Danil said, watching as she painted a tiny symbol onto a white patch of skin on his thumb. The ink had an iridescent gleam that reminded him of mage-crystals. A pleasant warmth immediately cut into the dull ache he'd felt since first touching the journal.

"Thank you," Danil said as sensation flooded back into his hand.

The young woman beamed at him. "I'm Elania, by the way. I was with you on the way in from the border," she said as she started on his other hand. "The snow leopard."

"Oh," he said. She didn't have the manner of a predator, but Danil supposed looks were deceiving.

"You're fortunate you didn't die when you touched the journal," Elania muttered, inspecting his forefinger with amber eyes. "My guess is they didn't expect anyone to steal it."

"I got lucky," he admitted.

"That's an understatement if ever I heard one." Elania dipped the paintbrush into the ink. "The mage who did the ice curse. Was it a woman? Dark hair turning grey, kinda scrawny, dresses in finery and talks like she only hangs out with dignified folk?"

Danil nodded in surprise. "Magus Brianna."

Elaina wrinkled her nose. "Figured as much. We've dealt with her before."

"You have?" Danil looked at her in astonishment. "Where?"

She sat back and eloquently spread her hands.

"In Amas," Danil concluded. Heart sinking, he realized Magus Brianna had broken the treaty. It explained why such a large party of Amasians patrolled the border. They were already prepared for war.

"Won't gaining the journal change things?" he asked desperately. "You don't have to declare war on Roldaer."

She tilted her head, amber eyes assessing. "Your Magus Brianna and her cohorts are rogues, Danil. It's what happens when a mage has too much wealth and influence." She sniffed. "We've no interest in war. We'll deal with her the same way we've dealt with treaty-breakers in the past."

Danil glanced at the bear shifter patrolling just beyond the edge of the camp. Its dark eyes gleamed in the firelight.

He shifted uncomfortably. "I broke the treaty, too."

"Not exactly," Elania said, looking up. "You were invited."

Danil followed her gaze to where Hafryn stood with his fists resting upon his hips. He spoke to the dragon as an equal, tapping at something in the journal. Sonnen listened closely, tilting his head in acquiescence. Used to the trickster side of the wolf, Danil found Hafryn's ability to command attention strangely compelling.

As if sensing eyes on him, the wolf shifter glanced up.

Danil quickly averted his gaze, feeling his cheeks grow warm.

Elania gave a low hum and continued to inscribe tiny symbols onto Danil's hands. A faint vibration could be felt under each symbol, growing stronger as she continued her work.

"What's so important about that journal, anyway?" Danil asked. He'd assumed the shifters would have been more alarmed by the presence of the mages and their personal guards in Farin. But the varying reactions of surprise and dismay evident when Danil handed the journal to Sonnen indicated otherwise.

The young woman hesitated, dark eyes conflicted. "It's very old—a Great War relic, in fact. As for what's inside, it's not my place to say."

Danil glanced again at Hafryn reading over the dragon prince's shoulder. "Magus Brianna was using it to find something in the deadlands. And in Altonas."

Elania made a noncommittal noise. "Altonas was destroyed in the Great War. There's nothing left but ruins."

"Well, something in that journal was enough to bring Magus Brianna to Farin," Danil replied. "And she ordered everyone away from Farin so that no one could see what she was up to."

"Yeah, about that," Elania began. She sat back, grimacing slightly. "Don't you think it odd that they all up and left without you? The villagers, I mean."

He did. But he also knew common folk didn't gamble with their lives by disputing a mage's orders.

"We can discuss the villagers later," a deep voice declared.

Danil glanced up to see Sonnen make his way around

the campfire. The same feeling of being prey stole into him as the shifter approached. Danil wondered if it had something to do with having a dragon contained within a human form. Hafryn paced behind Sonnen, green eyes bright.

"What's your assessment?" Sonnen asked, glancing at Elania.

Elania rose, dusting her hands on her breeches. "Danil's fine, for the most part. Biggest risk now is deadland poisoning from some scrapes, but the glyphs should take care of those, too."

Danil threw Hafryn a dour look as he clambered to his feet. They both knew just how he'd gotten those deadland scrapes.

The wolf scratched the side of his nose, his mouth quirking.

Sonnen turned back to Danil. "I've not thanked you fully for the information you brought us, Danil of Farin. We're in your debt."

Danil rubbed the back of his neck. "Thank you," he said awkwardly. "I—the soldiers might have followed me into Amas."

The dragon prince nodded. "We've panthers guarding the border. No one will slip past," he said.

Relief eased the tension across his shoulders. "Thank you," he murmured.

"It's not often that a human comes to us for sanctuary," Sonnen continued. "Nonetheless, you have it. Come morning, you and I will talk more about your place here in Amas, should you seek it."

"I'd like that," Danil replied.

"In the meantime, it is late and I'm certain you're weary

from your journey. Dawn is some time away. Hafryn can show you a place where you can clean up and refresh."

The wolf winked. "This way, Danil," he said, beckoning.

Danil sketched an awkward half-bow to Sonnen and followed, feeling the eyes of many shifters upon him as he trod across the camp.

THEY WORDLESSLY STRODE between the tents until Hafryn stopped at one dyed dark forest green. The wolf pulled back the tent flap and indicated for Danil to duck inside.

Soft light emanated from lamps set about the tent, the ground covered with plush, ornately woven rugs. A single oversized pallet lay in one corner, a heavily-scrolled wooden chest positioned at the foot of the bedding. In front of a curtained alcove was a veritable collection of cushions piled together like a nest.

Hafryn opened the chest and pulled out a clean tunic and breeches. "Here," he said, handing them over. "Bathing tub is behind the alcove. There's glyphs that keep the water clean and hot. But be sure to use the soapsand. The deadlands has a particular smell to it."

Danil thumbed the homespun cloth, finding the tunic softened and well worn. It was too large for him, but a perfect fit for Hafryn. Danil eyed the wolf. Used to seeing him naked, Danil was surprised at how the mottled tunic the shifter wore hinted at the muscle and lean planes underneath.

Hafryn noticed the intensity of his look. "What?"

Danil felt himself flush. "I've never seen you clothed before."

Hafryn folded his arms, looking Danil up and down. "Well, I've never seen you naked." He grinned in challenge.

Danil rolled his eyes. "That wasn't an invitation, wolf."

Hafryn raised his hands, chuffing. "Fine. I swear not to peek." He ambled over to the pile of cushions and threw himself down, wiggling to get comfortable. Tucking his hands behind his head, he smirked to see Danil still watching him. "Take your time. To get cleaned up, that is."

Muttering a curse, Danil went behind the alcove. There was indeed a simple wooden tub upon a platform, with steam rising off the water's surface. Plush towels and a robe hung off a nearby stand. A small side table sat beside the tub, a wine goblet within easy reach.

"Figures you'd be all about your own comfort," Danil muttered under his breath. It was far beyond anything he expected for a tent in the middle of nowhere.

The wolf shifter called out, "You should try my pallet. Only the finest bedding and silks."

"I'll pass, thanks."

Hafryn chuckled.

Danil loosened the ties to his tunic and tugged it free before kicking off his boots. He eyed the curtain before shucking off his breeches and quickly hopping into the tub. Heated water made him sigh in bliss as his muscles relaxed. After a short while, he grabbed a handful of soapsand and began working away the grime.

He froze before yanking his hands out of the water with a splash.

The symbols!

He checked his fingers only to see the litttle inscriptions still sharply defined on his skin.

"They're called glyphs, *fala*," Hafryn said, clearly having heard his surprised gasp. "They won't fade until their task is complete."

Tilting his hand, Danil watched the glyphs change color in the light. The skin underneath was a healthy pink. Then his eyes narrowed. "What did you just call me?"

Hafryn moved on the cushions. "What? *Fala*? It means moonflower."

"*Moonflower*?"

Hafryn huffed. "The moon calls to me, and you're pretty. Like a flower. So, moonflower. I figure we're at a point in our relationship where pet names are permissible."

Danil gaped at the curtain. "We're not—"

"You came to me in your time of need," Hafryn said reasonably.

"You *grabbed* me!"

"The details are open to interpretation," the wolf allowed, voice grudging. "But there are places in the deadlands where you could have stayed hidden for a time. You needn't run for Amas."

That was the truth right there. He sank down in the water to his earlobes. While he didn't want to see Roldaer and Amas at war, it wasn't exactly his duty to intervene. He wasn't quite ready to explore why he'd thought Amas was his best ally in stopping it.

Shaking his thoughts loose, he sat up and focused on scrubbing his arms with the soapsand. "How did you even know where to find me?"

Hafryn hummed in contemplation. "Instinct, I suppose. Plus you make enough noise for a herd of buffalo."

Danil rolled his eyes at the exaggeration. "Well, I'm grateful, anyway." He rinsed off the suds.

"The magi weren't keen to let you escape," Hafryn said. "And not solely, I suspect, because you stole the journal from right under their noses." He sounded rather jovial at that. "Do you have any idea what the magi meant when they spoke about an entrance?"

Danil rose out of the tub, shivering from the cold air. "A tunnel, maybe?" He quickly dried himself off. "Most of the mineshafts have collapsed, though, and the ones that remain are dangerous. I try to avoid going down there if I can."

"Common sense, do you think, or a compulsion?" Hafryn mused.

Danil pulled the clean tunic over his head. He wondered that himself. Some places he avoided more than others. He pulled on the breeches and tied the lacing closed. "Could there really be anything left down there? Some of those tunnels go deep." He stepped out from behind the alcove.

Hafryn lounged amongst the cushions. "The magi seem to think so, and that's enough for us." He looked Danil up and down. "You look much better," he said approvingly.

Danil smoothed down his tunic. "Not so scrappy, huh?"

Hafryn shrugged. "I like you scrappy."

The tent flap swung open to reveal Elania and a huge bear of a man. Both carried an armful of blankets.

"What's this?" Hafryn asked, rising.

"Sonnen's ordered that we spend the night in here," Elania said with a shrug. She dumped her bundle on the opposite side of the room. Her silent companion lowered his with more care.

"You think that's necessary?" Hafryn asked.

The young woman shrugged apologetically. "We'll do our best not to wake you when we come in later," she said to Danil.

"Thanks," he murmured.

Elania strode back outside. The man gave them both a polite nod before trailing after her.

A sour ball churned in Danil's belly. The dragon might have said earlier he was indebted, but it was obvious enough that the Amasians didn't trust him.

Hafryn seemed to share similar thoughts. He watched the tent flap swing back and forth, his expression contemplative.

6

Danil woke curled under a nest of blankets. He lay still for a moment, uncertain of where he was and why he'd woken. Glancing across the gloomy expanse of the tent, he spied Hafryn on his pallet. The wolf shifter snored softly, an embroidered pillow hugged tight to his chest. The two remaining pallets for Elania and her companion remained empty, despite the late hour. Hafryn made a snuffle and rolled onto his other side.

Outside the tent, the camp was quiet beyond the crackle of a campfire and the low murmur of voices speaking in Amasian. An owl hooted far in the distance.

Danil released a slow sigh, feeling a mix of uncertainty and displacement well up in his throat. He knew he couldn't go back to Roldaer, not with the magi certain to kill him. But he wasn't entirely sure he could go forward, either.

The tiny symbols on his skin glowed iridescent green then pink. Danil half-expected them to be gone by now, but they appeared sharply defined as if freshly painted. Wiggling his fingers made the symbols turn blue and silver.

Unable to sleep, Danil peeled back the blankets and padded across to the tent flap.

Easing it back, he saw a shifter guarding the entrance. She met his gaze before turning back to watch over the camp. The surrounding trees creaked softly as a pre-dawn breeze swept through. The firelight cast long shadows on the bark and moss.

Dozens of glowing eyes stared back at him from the dark of the forest.

Danil quickly closed the flap, heart thundering.

"Danil?"

Hafryn was already on his feet, hair mussed and sword in his hand.

"What is it?" the wolf asked.

Just some shifters, Danil thought sheepishly.

Rubbing the back of his neck, he said, "Nothing. I— sorry to have woken you," he said. He idly noted that the wolf shifter was fully dressed, boots too. "Do you normally sleep like that?"

Hafryn sheathed his sword. "You should get more sleep," he murmured.

Biting his lip, Danil nodded. He went to his makeshift pallet and sat, idly playing with the loose lacings at the neck of his tunic. The tunic felt soft on his skin, quite unlike the rough homespun he was used to. It was made for Hafryn's broader frame, though, and tended to slide off one shoulder.

Hafryn sat on the chest at the foot of Danil's pallet, sheathed sword resting across his knees.

Danil eyed the wolf, who stared back unblinkingly. "You're going to watch me sleep," he surmised with a sigh.

"It's no hardship, *fala,*" Hafryn said. His mouth turned up in that familiar, mischievous smile, but the night softened it somehow.

Danil felt his eye twitch at the pet name.

"Sonnen will fly you to Corros later today," Hafryn continued. "It's the largest citadel this side of the Igrett River. And a few days of flight by dragon's wing."

A shifter citadel...

Danil tested it in his mind but found himself wholly unable to imagine such a place.

"Will you be coming?" It was out before Danil could stop himself.

"I'm afraid not." Hafryn's mouth pulled down. "But thanks to you, we've got an inkling of what those two magi are up to."

Danil picked at a corner of his blanket. "Elania said Magus Brianna had already broken the treaty."

Hafryn grunted. "About six months ago. She was alone here on the borderlands and trying for stealth and secrecy. At the time we judged it best to keep an eye on her rather than send her back to Anteran with a stern missive for your king."

Danil recalled the sizeable private force she'd brought to Farin. "Do you truly think King Liam doesn't know what she's up to?" he asked.

Hafryn sighed. "The magi have always hungered for power. I don't believe your king shares their sentiment. Roldaer is prosperous, with a strong trading partnership with the Natalan Empire. War with Amas would gain King Liam little."

"Brianna thinks something lies within Altonas that's more powerful than a dragon."

"Then she's never met Sonnen." Hafryn tapped the engraved lines along the sheath of his sword. "Regardless, I'll feel better knowing you're safe in Corros."

Startled, Danil studied the wolf's face. There was a

tightness about his eyes that Danil had never seen before. "I'd rather stay here and help figure out what the magi have planned."

"No, not with what you know."

"But you know the deadlands just as well as I do!"

"I've never gone into the mines. They're too dark and—" Hafryn shuddered. "No. It's too risky for you to stay. Don't you want to be safe, Danil?"

Words lodged in his throat. He didn't know what he wanted. He couldn't even say he wanted things to go back to how they were just a few days ago, when Roldaer hadn't been on the cusp of war and he'd not known Hafryn preferred to sleep amid a nest of pillows.

Hafryn sighed. "In truth, I asked Sonnen to take you to Corros."

"What? *Why?*"

The wolf paused, green eyes searching. "Do you really not know?"

Danil froze, snared by Hafryn's gaze. He suspected he did know; he was just entirely unsure what to do about it.

The wolf released a sigh. "Listen, *fala*, I—"

The unmistakable clash of swords rang outside the tent.

Danil threw back the blankets, muscles tensing as the entrance flap yanked open.

A soldier in a familiar blue tabard burst inside. Already on his feet, Hafryn rushed to meet her. His sword struck hers with a resounding clash.

The attacker bore a strangely wooden expression as she parried Hafryn's second blow. Hafryn slashed at her again, teeth bared, but with a flurry of her cloak and a flash of green, she winked out of sight.

Hafryn cursed, whirling about. "Stay close, Danil," he

ordered. He pulled a dagger from his boot and handed it to him. "Be ready."

Danil gripped the small blade tightly, palm sweaty. "How did she do that?" he gasped, scanning about the tent even as specks of green drifted to the ground.

Hafryn shook his head, turning about to study each corner of the tent. "Mage-touched filth," he muttered.

A hooded figure materialized into being above Danil amid a crackle of green light. The attacker dropped down in front of him.

The man's face was emotionless, his movements stuttering but lightning quick as he snatched hold of Danil's tunic.

Danil stabbed blindly, only for the blade to skitter across hardened leather armor.

Hafryn leapt. From one heartbeat to the next, he transformed into a massive red wolf and pounced. Powerful teeth tore at the attacker's throat. The man fell without a sound.

Launching off him, Hafryn transformed mid-air back into human form, rolling to pick up his sword. He spat to clear the blood from his mouth.

A series of green flashes erupted above them. Hafryn became the wolf once again, springing to meet the first blank-faced attacker who soundlessly dropped down.

Hands suddenly grabbed a fistful of Danil's tunic. He stabbed again, feeling the dagger bite deep. His attacker didn't so much as grunt, instead bodily lifting Danil off his feet.

He stared into unseeing brown eyes, the man's face eerily vacant.

"*No more running, guide,*" Magus Brianna's voice rang from the man's lips.

Green flecks amassed about them. The air buzzed.

The man suddenly stiffened, and Danil heard a solid thud. Two more thuds followed in rapid succession. The green light abruptly dissipated, and the man pitched forward, releasing Danil as he struck the ground.

Danil whirled.

Elania stood at the entrance, her hand raised as a glyph shot across the tent to take down another intruder. Blue smoke coiled up from the resulting burn in the man's chest.

Then a huge black bear barreled past Elania. With a terrible roar, it swiped an attacker with a huge paw. The hooded woman flew across the tent to strike the canvas and soundlessly crumple to the ground.

Hafryn shifted and rolled before striking down another with his blade.

The air above them coalesced with sparks of green. Danil tightened his grip on the bloodied dagger. Hafryn slid in front of him, sword ready.

"Wards!" Elania shouted.

The bear transformed into the silent man Danil had seen earlier in the night. He wove his hand in the air, an odd symbol taking shape. Elania created the same; the symbols streaked across the tent and through the walls to outside.

A hum filled the air, rapidly followed by a scream from a woman who sounded startlingly like Magus Brianna. The remaining green flecks floated to the dirt and disappeared.

"Blutark, hold the wards," Elania ordered the bear shifter.

The sound of battle outside continued, with flashes of green and orange fire lighting the tent walls. Then a dragon released a massive roar of triumph. The ground vibrated with an unseen energy, and then an eerie silence followed.

Dry mouthed, Danil waited for long heartbeats until

Amasian voices filled the quiet. Unrushed footsteps sounded outside, along with the tread of animals as they checked the perimeter.

Blutark watched with dark eyes as Elania bent over one of the fallen attackers to inspect something on his belt. She summoned a magelight, washing the tent in a warm glow.

Hafryn slid his sword into its sheath. "That went pretty much as expected," he muttered, wiping his bloodied mouth with the edge of his tunic.

Danil glanced at him, startled. A cold lump lodged in his throat.

As expected...

They'd somehow known the attack would happen. And yet they'd left him in a tent with only one fighter for protection.

Understanding settled heavily in Danil's stomach. He forced his face to remain expressionless as he gazed about at the shifters, hyperaware of his own humanity and expendability.

The shifters had dangled him like a tasty morsel to draw in the magi.

And they'd probably do it again.

7

A handful of shifters came to drag the bodies out of the tent. Danil numbly stood by the alcove to stay out of the way, watching as Hafryn gave orders while dressing in a fresh tunic and breeches from the upturned chest. The wolf looked annoyed by the disarray, cursing at the spatter of blood on his embroidered cushions.

"Danil, come look at this," Elania called from where she crouched over an attacker.

He approached on heavy feet.

She pulled up the sleeve of the dead man's tunic. A thin layer of ice crystals coated the skin. "Magi-touched," she muttered, then spat on the ground. "Some soldiers give themselves over to be used as puppets by their magi masters. It makes them stronger and faster, but there's a cost."

Danil shivered, recalling the way the wooden-faced attackers had died without a sound.

"At least the cost to the magi is even greater," Elania continued. "Your magi will be drained for days."

"One of them spoke," Danil said dully. "It sounded like Magus Brianna."

Elania's gaze intensified. "What did she say?"

Hafryn came to stand beside her. "'No more running'," the wolf said, face grim. "They came for him, Elania. Not just for the journal. I warned Sonnen of this."

The woman's expression became difficult to read. "We have the wards to stop the magi from transporting more soldiers into camp. All will be well."

A slow anger built in Danil's guts. If such wards existed, they could have stopped the soldiers from arriving in the first place.

Hafryn studied him, green eyes dark with concern. "Are you well, *fala*? "

Danil clenched his teeth. "What do you care?"

Hafryn frowned and stepped close. "Of course I care—"

Danil struck Hafryn's jaw with a loud crack. The wolf shifter staggered back, shock on his face.

"You used me as bait!" Danil shouted.

Blutark was there in a heartbeat to pull Danil back with an arm about the throat.

He hardly cared. He launched himself at Hafryn as the wolf rubbed his jaw. "You bastard! You knew the magi would send soldiers after me!"

The bear shifter dragged him back a few steps.

"Danil—" Hafryn began.

"Don't lie to me," Danil snarled. "You slept with your boots on! You don't even wear clothes in the deadlands!"

Hafryn had the grace to look chagrined. "I can explain."

"What? How funny it is to dupe the human?"

The wolf frowned. "No. Never that, Danil."

"Right. And I'm supposed to trust your word." Danil pushed at the arm about his throat. "Let go!"

The tent flap snapped back to reveal Sonnen. He stepped inside, his eyes gleaming dangerously in the magelight.

"That's enough," the dragon prince ordered.

Danil refused to be cowed. "Stuff you and your sanctuary," he spat at Sonnen. "You used me to kill Roldaerian soldiers!"

"*Enough!*" the dragon roared.

It vibrated through to Danil's bones. He froze, teeth clenched, but kept his heated gaze locked on the dragon.

"Leave us," Sonnen ordered.

Blutark released his grip on Danil and trailed after Elania, who sent Danil a concerned look before striding out of the tent.

"You, too, Hafryn."

Mouth thinning, the wolf shifter gave a short nod and followed the pair.

Danil curled his hands into fists as footfalls faded away.

Sonnen clasped his hands behind his back. "Will you listen to my words, or has your rage not yet run its course?"

Jaw tightening, Danil said, "Why should I hear anything you say?"

The dragon studied him, golden eyes unreadable. "My enchanters were with you, along with my best warrior. The magi were never going to have you."

Danil remembered the green light buzzing about him to transport him away. That Hafryn would endanger him, so too this dragon despite his promise of safety...

He swallowed, heartsick and at a loss.

His thoughts must have shown on his face for Sonnen released a sigh. "You brought a journal only the mageborn can touch, Danil of Farin. Despite Hafryn's assurances, we couldn't be sure you weren't a magi trap."

"A trap." Danil stared at him bleakly. "I'd have thought it obvious that I'm no mage. They want to kill me."

"The magi have set elaborate ruses in the past. I won't apologize for my caution."

Danil's shoulders slumped. Cold bitterness settled in his belly. He'd risked everything to thwart the magi's plans, but was now trapped and at this dragon's mercy.

"For what it's worth, however, I believe you."

Danil squinted up at him.

Sonnen sighed deeply. "I would have sensed a mage walking the deadlands all these seasons. Added to that is Hafryn—he speaks well of you."

A tangled heat filled Danil's belly. "Oh," he managed.

"As for bringing the journal, you wouldn't have survived the ice curse without some measure of untapped potential."

The very idea of him having any magic was ludicrous. "I was born in Farin," Danil argued. "My family has lived and died beside the deadlands for generations. We're very aware of our lack of potential."

"It's possible the deadlands quietened your innate abilities. Enchantments rarely flourish there." Sonnen frowned, flame-filled eyes contemplative. "From what I can tell, your gift is limited. Nonetheless, there is something about you..."

Danil shifted under the intensity of the dragon's regard.

Sonnen shook his head to clear it, then seemed to come to some sort of decision. "I ask that you don't judge Hafryn too harshly. He argued against tonight's plan, and when I wouldn't change it, he insisted you stay here."

Hurt flared again. "He could have warned me." In a kingdom full of strangers, he'd trusted Hafryn. Blindly so.

"Would you, in his place?"

Danil folded his arms, discomforted. "I don't like being manipulated," he muttered.

Sonnen's mouth quirked. "Noted." He pointed to Danil's hands. "May I?"

Frowning, Danil raised his left hand. The dragon turned it palm-up. The glyphs on his fingertips appeared blurred on the edges and no longer glittered so brightly.

Sonnen sighed. "I'm afraid there are other matters we were not forthcoming about, Danil of Farin."

"How so?" Danil asked, not particularly surprised.

"These glyphs are not only for healing, but also served to warn us of a farseeking."

With a sinking feeling, Danil said, "I don't understand."

The dragon muttered an unfamiliar word, and the glyphs brightened once more. "The ice curse left a mark that goes far deeper than frostbite," Sonnen said. He released Danil's hand. "It makes you...traceable. At least to the mage who created the ice curse."

His heart skipped a beat. "You mean Magus Brianna can find me."

"As long as she lives, yes. My intent to take you to Corros is to hide you from her. Earlier tonight I didn't know if you were her apprentice or her enemy, but the results are the same. There are enough enchantments in the citadel to mask your presence."

"But not out here."

"I'll take you to Corros, if that's your wish," Sonnen said, his eyes intent. "But I'd prefer if you made your way to Altonas."

That wasn't what he was expecting. His eyes narrowed. "The broken citadel? Why? Brianna and Ronan are heading there."

"I won't lie; it'll be dangerous," Sonnen said. "But you won't travel alone."

Danil stared at him with growing dread. "Why would I want to go there at all? I don't even know how to hold a sword! And if Magus Brianna can find me—" A shudder went through him. "You want me as bait again," he said bleakly.

"It's your choice, Danil. Altonas is abandoned and of no significance. For some reason, two Roldaerian mages desire it. We must find out why."

"But my going there will just warn them that I've told you everything."

"I would prefer all eyes on Altonas."

Danil's eyes narrowed. "Because of the journal."

Sonnen quirked an eyebrow.

He flushed. "Brianna wouldn't have cursed it because she hates to share," he pointed out.

The dragon smiled slightly. "That's highly debatable. But, yes, the journal once belonged to a powerful enemy of Amas. That his work fell into the hands of a mage is deeply troubling."

"Who was he?"

"His name was Kaul," Sonnen said. Flames gathered in his golden eyes. "And he created the deadlands."

8

A dozen bodies lay strewn about the camp. No shifters were among the dead, although some lay injured. Danil trailed after Sonnen, seeing an bloodied sparrow being tended to by an elderly man. The sparrow's harsh breaths eased as glyphs brightened on one tawny wing.

Danil slowed at the sight of a Roldaerian soldier kneeling between two shifters, her arms bound behind her back. The soldier noticed Danil and smirked, the movement pulling at a fresh cut at her mouth. The pin above her breast glinted in the gathering light.

"Do you recognize her?" Sonnen asked, pausing at his side.

"I—yes." The bruises on his ribs flared to life. "That's Commander Voss. She arrived in Farin with Magus Brianna."

With a thin smile, Sonnen indicated to the shifter guards to drag the commander to her feet. The shifters walked her to the trees. Commander Voss seemed hardly to care, head held high.

"What are you going to do to her?" Danil asked,

watching as the commander and her escort disappeared into the forest. Unease coiled in his belly.

"As a mage's commander, she will likely know more than most. That the magus entrusted her with retrieving Kaul's journal says much."

Danil glanced at him in surprise.

The dragon's eyes were slitted flames as he gazed about the camp. "Your Magus Brianna underestimated our preparedness. I suspect she will not make the same mistake again." He motioned with his hand. "This way." He stalked onto a path between two tents.

Danil hurried to stay apace with the dragon's long strides. "The man who created the deadlands," he began. "Kaul. He—I didn't think anyone could have such power."

To think just one man could scorch the earth bare for centuries. Danil shuddered.

"He didn't," Sonnen said. "Not within himself, at least. His ability to manipulate kiandrite—what you call mage-crystals—and store their power made him a terrible adversary. It was luck that the deadlands aren't far larger."

They entered a new tent. It looked like a storeroom, with a series of shelves laden with items like water flagons, trailbread, daggers and boots. A significant array of tunics and breeches were also on hand.

To Danil's surprise, Hafryn was busily stuffing a cloak and other items into a pack. The wolf paused when he noticed their entry. He met Danil's gaze with something like guilt in his eyes.

"You okay?" Hafryn asked. A larger question seemed hidden beneath it.

Danil managed a nod. He raised a hand to show the glyphs. "Ready to be spied upon once again," he said dourly.

Hafryn quirked an eyebrow and turned to the dragon.

"You told Danil about the farseeking. I suppose that means you've drawn a new conclusion about him?"

A deep growl came from Sonnen's chest. "The night's outcome was not a surprise to me."

"Really?" Hafryn snorted. He sat back on his heels, expression troubled. "That was no small incursion, my friend. We've not seen an attack of that ilk in a long time. A *very* long time."

"I know it," Sonnen muttered. "It's possible more mages are involved than we first thought."

Hafryn hummed thoughtfully. "Magus Brianna may be wealthy enough to influence other mages to her cause while staying beneath King Liam's notice."

Sonnen slid golden eyes toward Danil. "Did you notice anything of the sort?"

Danil shook his head. "I saw only Ronan and Brianna. And the guards at Farin all carried Brianna's insignia."

Hafryn gave a frustrated sigh. "At least we have Kaul's journal, even if the latter sections are magicked."

Danil rubbed his arms. "Is it the ice curse?"

Sonnen made a sound of negation. "The enchantment is quite old—a working of Kaul himself, I believe. The words slide about the page and make little sense." His golden eyes showed flames. "Given time I will know its contents."

"Might want to hurry, Sonnen," Hafryn said, shoving a handful of tunics into his pack. "To show their hand so soon, I'd almost say the magi are panicking."

Sonnen nodded. "I've sent word to Corros for a squadron to meet you at the broken citadel. In the meantime, you should prepare another pack."

Hafryn tilted his head. "For who?" He glanced at Danil before scowling. "No. You gave your word, Sonnen!"

"Danil was given a choice. He chose to join you in Altonas."

Danil hid his surprise. Joining Hafryn hadn't exactly been disclosed.

The wolf's lip curled as he rose to his feet. "He'll be safer in Corros."

"He will," Sonnen agreed reasonably. "But he knows the risks."

Hafryn laughed sourly. "Does he?" He turned to Danil. "I saw how you fight, Danil. What if another soldier grabs you? What if a *mage* takes you?"

"Elania and Blutark are going with you," Sonnen said.

"As they should be! But not as personal guards for a cursed human!" Hafryn yelled.

Danil scowled. "Is that what I am to you? A cursed human?"

Hafryn scrubbed his hair in frustration. "Not in the way you're taking it, *fala*," he muttered.

Danil folded his arms. "I get the feeling nowhere is safe for me right now," he murmured. "Besides, if I'm in Altonas, Brianna herself is likely to show up. You can catch her and break the curse, along with stopping whatever she has planned."

Hafryn swore. "You make it sound so easy."

He shrugged, ignoring the wolf's sarcasm.

Sonnen watched the exchange with amusement. "Don't gnaw on an old bone, Hafryn. The human has made his decision. It is an insult to demand he make another."

Hafryn shook his head. "I mean no insult, *fala*. I just know you've already done enough." He sighed at Danil's resolute expression. "But if you're intent on haring off through the mountains, I'd prefer it be with me." He pointed at Danil. "But that means you do as I say. No arguing!"

Danil nodded, trying not to smile. An unnamable weight lifted off his shoulders.

The wolf huffed. He turned back to Sonnen. "How many are joining us from here?"

"A squad of ten. The rest will remain here to patrol and watch over activities in Farin. I'll be taking the journal...elsewhere."

Hafryn nodded, unquestioning.

"I want you on the trail within the hour," Sonnen said.

The wolf gave him a lazy salute. "Will do, my prince." He glanced at Danil. "Pack what you need. Anything doesn't fit, I'm sure Sonnen can enchant it for you."

The dragon's mouth quirked. He bowed his head in agreement. "As you say, wolf."

Hafryn tied the top of his pack and without a word shouldered his way past Sonnen to exit the tent.

Danil stared after him. "I think he's angry with you."

"It'll pass," Sonnen murmured. "Just don't get yourself hurt or I'll never hear the end of it."

Danil felt strangely heartened by that.

9

They travelled along the banks of a river as it weaved deep through forest and gorges. The snow-covered mountains loomed high overhead, casting long shadows throughout the day.

Danil trod the single-file path on quiet feet. The shifters took up a hard pace, navigating the steep riverbank with ease. Hafryn strode a few paces ahead, his red braid swinging jauntily back and forth. Other shifters kept to their animal forms, slinking along the darkened tree line. Elania in particular seemed to melt into the dappled sunlight, her spotted leopard coat blending with the rich soil. Danil supposed her silent companion, Blutark, was somewhere further in the trees, having remained unseen since they set out.

The sun indicated mid-morning as they made their way down a series of escarpments. A waterfall roared beside them, making the rocks slippery with damp. At the bottom, the river fed out into a large basin that looked ideal for swimming. A few shifters paused to refill their waterskins.

Danil joined Hafryn at the water's edge. He eased down

his pack and stretched out the knots along his spine. Sprawling beech trees sank their heavy roots into the water on the opposite bank. Danil watched a single leaf spiral down to land on the cool surface.

"Is all of Amas like this?" he wondered.

"Mountainous, you mean?" The wolf handed him a waterskin.

Danil nodded. "I've never travelled beyond Farin, but I know Roldaer is mostly flat land. A soldier once told me that there are provinces where they grow little more than grains, and at summer the whole land is a big field of yellow."

Hafryn grunted. "We have our farming provinces, though hardly on the scale you speak of. Most Amasians crave wildness, so we have a care over how we treat our lands. Even the peat bogs and marshes are sacred to many clans." He smiled. "We all manage to get along."

"What clan was Kaul from?" Danil asked.

Hafryn's smile fell. "A large one. But he's dead, thank the stars."

Danil resisted the urge to roll his eyes. "That's a given, considering he was in the Great War." He took a large gulp from the waterskin, relishing the coolness in his throat.

Hafryn eyed him. "Some Amasians live longer than others," he said as he took back the waterskin. "As a halfbreed, however, Kaul wasn't so blessed. Nor was he particularly smart, considering he sided with the human magi."

"I didn't know there were halfbreeds," Danil said as he collected his pack. They started along the river once more.

"Kaul was the first and to my knowledge the only halfbreed. Our two kinds don't seem to mix so well, at least not when the goal is childbearing." Hafryn's mouth slanted upwards. He stepped over a fern wedged into the rock. "Kaul had a magical bent that allowed him to manipulate kiandrite. He experimented in ways that are anathema to Amasians."

"Like the magi," Danil murmured, thinking of Ronan's firewhip.

Hafryn nodded. "The journal is one of Kaul's earlier works. He really didn't perfect kiandrite manipulation until he was well into his sixties, and his earlier experiments required significant quantities of kiandrite. Which is likely why the magi plan to invade Altonas."

"But what's so important about the citadel?"

"It's both Kaul's birthplace and where he died, so it makes sense that the magi think he left something there. As a youngster, Kaul was particularly adept at channeling kiandrite into glass orbs. We know that an orb of corruption resulted in the abandonment of Altonas. Another orb might still exist in the ruins, but—" Hafryn tilted his hand back and forth.

"It should have been discovered by now," Danil surmised. The thought of the magi accessing that much power left him chilled.

"It's not all bad. Altonas was once a large citadel. The magi will have a lot of ground to cover. And we'll be there to meet them."

Danil hardly looked forward to it, but pressed on regardless.

LATER THAT AFTERNOON, a bitter coldness swept over the back of Danil's neck. It felt much like the icy winds that moaned across the deadlands in the dark of winter.

A stillness took over the forest. Not even a whisper of breeze stirred the branches. The soft pad of footfalls marked the crossing of a small rodent in the underbrush. A shifter in the form of white-tailed dove winged overhead as she marked the trail for them to follow. Hafryn talked quietly with two other shifters as they moved amidst the trees.

The coldness swept across Danil once more. His skin pebbled as the feeling of being watched stole over him.

A sudden image flashed across his vision of Magus Brianna. She sat in the inn's aleroom, bowed over a silver bowl. Gossamer-thin spears of ice spread out across the floor beneath her slippered feet like a spider's web.

Danil shook his head to clear it.

The air directly above him seemed greyed somehow, congealing by the moment. Danil stared until it seemed like a pair of pale blue eyes stared back at him through the cloud.

'*Found you, guide,*' Brianna whispered in his mind.

"Danil!"

Elania emerged from amongst the trees. Iridescent glyphs showed brightly on dark skin as she raised her hand. A powerful force shot through the trees and struck the cloud with a thunderous crack.

Danil was lifted off his feet and flung across the gully. He crashed into the leaf mold, the breath knocked out of him.

A woman's maddened chortle echoed in the distance. The cloud rapidly broke apart and disappeared.

Hafryn slid to a halt beside Danil. He grabbed his face with both hands. "Danil!"

"I'm fine," he gasped out. He struggled up onto his elbows, his lungs burning.

"Cursed magi filth," Hafryn snarled, looking murderous.

Elania and Blutark crouched beside them. The young

woman had the grace to look guilty. "Forgive me, Danil. I misjudged what would happen when I broke the connection."

Danil wiped his mouth with a shaking hand. "What was that?"

"A farseeking," Blutark growled, his voice a deep baritone. "Normally the magi aren't so obvious about it."

Elania nodded. "That cloud. She wanted us to know her business. Did you see those eyes?" She shivered.

Danil wheezed as Hafryn helped him sit upright and dusted his back for dirt. "But I already knew she was spying on us." He told them what he'd felt and seen.

"How unexpected," Elania murmured.

Blutark studied Danil's face, dark eyes curious. "A reverse seeking isn't an apprentice's trick. You shouldn't be able to perform it."

Danil stared at him in bewilderment.

"A side effect of the ice curse?" Hafryn asked, worried.

Blutark looked thoughtful. "The purpose of farseeking is to remain hidden. That Magus Brianna made herself visible is likely to taunt you, Danil. But I can't imagine she'd want her own location known as well."

Elania studied his face. "You must warn us next time."

Danil bit the inside of his cheek. He hardly wanted to be blasted off his feet again.

Hafryn grinned, having read something from Danil's expression. "Come on, up you get." He gripped Danil's forearm and heaved him to his feet. "Let's get some distance from here, eh?"

Blutark fished out Danil's pack from where it lay tossed amidst the ferns.

Danil murmured his thanks. He ached everywhere. "I

thought Magus Brianna couldn't do any magic after the attack last night."

"Farseeking isn't the same as transporting," Blutark said, watching as Elania started back up the trail. She shimmered and became a snow leopard. "There must have been a dusting of kiandrite in the bowl to augment her abilities." He hesitated, frowning. "It will likely get easier with time."

"You mean to find me?" Danil asked in alarm.

The bear shifter nodded. "That is the way of farseekings."

Danil struggled to push down his dismay.

Glancing at Hafryn, he saw worry also tighten the wolf's expression.

10

Magus Brianna looked in on Danil twice the following day. Each time, his skin prickled as if coated with hoarfrost moments before grey mist coalesced above him. The last farseeking occurred just as they set up camp for the night, and after a short discussion, the party decided to trek on into the darkness.

"She does it to rattle us," Hafryn muttered as they made a slow path through the underbrush. He eased back a low vine. "She thinks that by revealing each farseeking, our resolve will crumble, and we'll abandon you." His teeth showed whitely in the dimness. "To be clear, *fala,* that's not going to happen."

Moonlight filtered through the canopy to reveal vines, spindly climbers and an array of ferns, moss and liverworts amidst the foliage. A twig snapped nearby, and Danil caught sight of a pale arctic wolf as it padded along at the edge of the party.

Danil thought of the latest farseeking, when he'd caught vision of not just Brianna but three other mages in the aleroom. Two appeared to be making scratchings in workbooks, but the third waved a crystal that glowed weak orange over a piece of black quartz. Ronan was nowhere in sight.

He frowned. "What does it mean if they're using magic on deadland stones?"

Elania made a sound of negation behind him. "The deadlands are barren in life and energy. Enchantments won't work on it, no matter how powerful the enchanter or mage."

"So what was the orange crystal?" Danil asked.

"My guess is a scrying stone," Elania said. "They're trying to find their mysterious entrance."

"Must be pretty desperate to try enchantments on the deadlands itself," Hafryn said.

"If Kaul created the deadlands, is it possible he hid an orb there?" Danil asked.

The wolf frowned. "If he did, it was likely lost when he destroyed the leylines."

Danil tilted his head at the unfamiliar word.

Despite the darkness under the tree canopy, Hafryn must have read his confusion. "Leylines are ancient underground pathways. It's not unusual to find them near the likes of rivers, waterfalls, and hot springs—anywhere nature's energy is most evident. Even Roldaer has leylines, but only in Amas do kiandrite crystals form on their edges."

"But people used to mine for mage-crystals in the deadlands before it was tapped out," Danil argued.

Hafryn shook his head. "Later in life, Kaul grew interested in forcing Roldaerian leylines to produce kiandrite. He siphoned off the life force in a Amasian leyline and fed it into a Roldaerian one. That there was kiandrite in the deadlands indicates he had some measure of success, but blending the leylines created a cataclysmic reaction.

The explosion that created the deadlands would have also spewed kiandrite in every direction."

"Hence why kiandrite could be found at random," Danil mused, thinking of the haphazard warren of tunnels and mineshafts. "Nowadays, it's whatever the meltwater brings from the Amasian mountains."

"It's surprising that you're even able to find that much," Hafryn said, throwing him a curious look.

Danil shrugged. Desperation and fear were good motivators. "I usually—" He stopped at the brush of icy fingers across his skin.

Glancing up, he saw the air coalesce into grey light. An image of Brianna smiling as she leaned over a silver bowl flashed in his mind.

A bear shimmered out of the darkness to reveal Blutark. The man shot a bolt of silver at the cloud and watched grim-faced as Brianna's farseeking dissipated.

"Thanks," Danil managed.

Elania shared a look with the bear shifter. "I'll send warning to Sonnen about the extra mages."

Blutark nodded.

She stepped off the trail to allow the rest of the party to pass her. Cupping her hands, Elaina whispered something into her palms. A few moments later, a tiny spark of light burst free and shot away between the tree trunks back towards the border.

"We should keep moving," Blutark muttered.

Mouth thin, Hafryn indicated for Danil to follow. They had many hours of walking ahead of them.

THE FARSEEKINGS CONTINUED throughout the night and well

into the day. It seemed that whenever a respite felt possible, coldness swept over Danil and the cloud with its icy blue specter formed above the party. They'd not paused for more than a handful of moments since the previous day.

Weariness tugged at Danil's bones as he paused in front of a small ledge of rock, staring up with tired dislike. Elania shimmered into her snow leopard Trueform and launched up onto the ledge with a single, powerful jump. She transformed again and leaned down to offer her hand.

He mustered a smile and allowed himself to be heaved up. "Thanks," he murmured.

They walked together across the ledge to where it widened beside a large bed of yellow mushrooms.

"Don't be disheartened by the farseekings, yeah?" Elania said. Dirt streaked her cheek. "The magus does it to track us, but we have the upper hand. She doesn't know you can farsee her, too. That's power, Danil."

He tried to absorb that. If there was a chance to outwit Magus Brianna, he'd take it.

Elania winked, showing dimples. "You're not what I expected of humans. Kinda thought you'd fall behind by now."

Danil didn't take offence. He'd made certain assumptions about Amasians, also. But they weren't the strange, unwelcoming folk he'd feared. "There's plenty of things I don't get about Amasians," he said.

She threw him a curious look as they made their way across patches of snow clinging about the base of saplings and fernery. "Such as?"

"Okay," he said, running a few questions in his mind. "Why is it that you keep your clothes on when you shift back from your Trueform?"

Elania paused, dark eyes assessing.

Danil quickly raised his hands. "Hafryn never wore clothes in the deadlands," he added in a rush.

She abruptly snorted. "That wolf." Clearly trying not to laugh, she said, "We use glyphs to ensure we don't lose our clothes each time we shift."

"Really," he said, nonplussed.

She tapped a small, angular symbol on the inside of her elbow. "We learn to draw it as younglings. Of course, there are purists in the northern reaches who don't use the glyphs."

"I see." Danil glanced back at Hafryn as the wolf navigated his way up the ledge.

"Hafryn isn't one of them," she said, smirking despite the tiredness under her eyes. "If you've seen him naked, it's because he wanted you to."

Danil felt his cheeks burn.

Hafryn met his gaze as he crossed the stone ledge, green eyes mild.

He quickly turned back around, scowling. "Trickster wolf," he muttered under his breath.

Elania chuckled. "Trickster wolf, indeed."

11

The ambush came on a mountainous strip of the trail. A series of 'thwacks' had Danil wheeling about as objects struck the surrounding trees.

"Archers!" someone shouted.

The bolt wedged into the bark closest to Danil had a black shaft veined with kiandrite. The colors swirled and brightened a heartbeat before a white flash blinded him. A boom vibrated through his body and suddenly he pitched sideways. Screams and animal shrieks rang out.

Blinking rapidly, Danil saw a blurred figure reach him and haul him to his feet. Danil gripped the man's tunic, expecting on the edges of his vision to see a red braid.

"Hafryn—" he began, but then caught sight of white hair and pale blue eyes.

Ronan...

Flailing in a panic, Danil hit out with his fists. Magus Ronan's head snapped back, and suddenly a white-tailed dove with metal-sheathed talons raked across the mage's face. The mage screamed in fury.

Danil wrenched loose. His vision cleared to see blue-cloaked soldiers battling against various woodland creatures.

Green sparked about Magus Ronan as he reached for Danil once more. Three gouges scored the side of the mage's face. He grinned bloodily. "You're ours now."

A red wolf catapulted into the mage with a guttural snarl. The impact left Danil staggering. He lost his footing and tumbled head over foot down an embankment. His head struck a rock.

Blackness took him.

DANIL WOKE to the snap of twigs. Something charged through the underbrush. Dazed, he skittered back until he braced against a tangle of roots. The embankment loomed above him, with crushed undergrowth and disturbed snow showing his path down. No sounds of fighting echoed from on high.

A giant red wolf bounded over the thick brush. It saw Danil immediately and trotted over, making distressed whines.

Danil pressed his face into the creature's pale ruff. "I'm okay, Hafryn," he gasped out. The side of his face felt sticky with blood.

Hafryn transformed, green eyes worried as he inspected the wound in Danil's hairline. "That's a mighty bruise, *fala*." He gripped Danil's chin and studied his eyes with disconcerting intensity.

Danil gently pushed his hand away. "I said I'm fine, wolf."

Hafryn sat back on his heels. "We can't stay here. Can you walk?"

With a nod, he gripped Hafryn's forearm and let himself be helped upright. The world spun dizzyingly and then settled.

Hafryn watched him closely as he waited for the disorientation to pass. Then he motioned for Danil to start back up the embankment.

At the top, two of Magus Brianna's soldiers lay dead, but none of the Amasians had fallen. Strangely, Blutark and two other shifters crowded around a blonde-haired companion, who stood with her head bowed. She cried softly.

Danil threw Hafryn a worried glance.

Elania answered from where she sat strapping her arm with a bandage. "It's her little brother, Talis," she muttered, tying off the end of the bandage with a vicious tug. Shadows showed under her eyes. "They took him the moment the fight turned against them."

Danil gaped. "*What?*"

He tried to remember the shifter. Pale haired, tawny-eyed. His Trueform was a small mountain cat with a black tip on its tail.

"The magi have done it in the past," Hafryn said in a low murmur. He watched Blutark comfort the woman. "We don't know where our people go or what happens to them."

"Only that we never hear of them again," Elania spat. She rose to her feet, her dark eyes furious.

"I had no idea," Danil murmured, looking back at the weeping woman in horror. What would the magi want with Amasians?

Elania pointed with her chin. "You need healing?"

Danil touched his tender scalp. It was nothing in the scale of things. "I can keep going."

"Good." The snow leopard gathered her pack, before

picking up another that lay abandoned in the moss. She let out a whistle.

Blutark looked up and nodded. He murmured something to the woman and squeezed her shoulder. Moments later, she transformed into a panther and bolted from sight.

12

A t Hafryn's signal, Danil hunkered behind a fallen tree.

He peered between the leaves and caught a flash of pale blue amidst the greenery. He ducked down again.

Blutark crouched beside him, crossbow planted atop the frost-rimed bark. This close, Danil could see faint silvery flames writhe above the arrowhead.

The snap of twigs and undergrowth drew his attention back to the approaching soldiers. Every muscle tensed in preparation.

The first soldier marched past, vacant eyed and stony faced. Danil counted ten more soldiers before Magus Ronan stalked into view. Three long gouges marked his face from jaw to eyebrow. A cold fury showed in his eyes as he swept past the underbrush.

A dozen more soldiers flanked him. None appeared fatigued despite an unrelenting march which had lasted three days.

Danil and his companions waited for the crack of branches smashing underfoot to fade.

Hafryn eventually motioned. 'This way,' he mouthed before he slinked down into a small gully.

They headed west, where a rugged mountain peak heavy with snow was visible above the treeline.

Exhaustion pulled at Danil with every step, and he watched with envy as a few of the shifters stayed in their Trueforms simply to stay apace. He wasn't sure how much further he could go without rest.

Three days had passed since the ambush. Despite knowing the terrain, the shifters had been unable to shake Magus Ronan from their path. Blutark muttered darkly under his breath about enchantments designed to make magi-touched soldiers endure more than they should. Even at night, torches cast a mean glow amidst the spruce trees.

With a sense of guilt, Danil wondered if the Amasians could outrun Ronan's force if they all shifted.

"Some of us, yes," Hafryn murmured when he tentatively asked. They traversed a stream cleaving a gully in two. "But Castalan is a vole, and Enil's a badger—not conducive to running. In battle, however, I'd have them at my back any day."

A panther slinked ahead in the undergrowth before disappearing from view.

"Thankfully, we're close enough now to Altonas that we can avoid a battle," Hafryn added.

Danil almost sagged in relief. "We're close?"

"Half a day at most, Danil. Then we can discover what the magi are really up to."

~

MOSS-COVERED STONE CARVED in the shape of a serpent marked the edge of the citadel.

Trees grew thick and wild, with roots splayed over crumbling stone that were perhaps once towers and cobbled paths. Massive blocks of stone lay amongst clover as if tossed there by a giant. Vestiges of buildings were visible through the trees, along with moldering buttresses of intricate detail, some of which were still upright and entangled with vines. Danil looked up as he stepped under an archway stained dark and green. Small glyphs, smoothed to almost nothing, showed between the lichen.

A shifter brushed past him to murmur in Hafryn's ear. "We need to hurry."

Amidst the trees behind them, Danil caught a pale flash of a soldier's tabard. His shoulders sagged. "You've got to be kidding," he muttered.

Elania whispered into her hands. A spark of light shot out to race ahead through the ruins.

"This way," Hafryn said, breaking into a trot as he changed direction onto a dirt path lined with towering fir trees.

Danil glanced back to see that Ronan and the soldiers still followed. Even in the distance, he could see the deep cuts lining the mage's cheek. The soldiers about him fanned out, faces expressionless.

The citadel spread out across a trio of undulating hills and gullies, broken up by a craggy peak at its center. Trees, vines and undergrowth grew in wild abandon, masking the full breadth of the broken citadel sprawl. All about were relics of a past life, including tool-making, stone benches and even a hair pin inset with a red jewel lying abandoned under the wide fronds of an elkhorn.

"In here," Hafryn eventually said, ducking through a collapsed section of lichen-stained wall. They stepped into the remains of a small building, a tree in one corner stretching up past what was once the roof line.

Blutark strung his crossbow and found a gap in the stone-and-mud wall. He murmured under his breath, and a silvery flame licked across the surface of the bolt. Two other shifters joined Blutark, eyes intent on the path threading between the trees a few hundred feet away.

"Quietly," Hafryn murmured, motioning for everyone to play least in sight. He drew his sword with a slow hiss, then hunched down beside Danil against the crumbling stone.

Danil peered through a tiny gap in the stonework.

A few heartbeats later, pale blue amidst the greenery caught his eye. Five Roldaerian soldiers pushed through the undergrowth, their faces devoid of emotion. Magus Ronan stalked behind them. Another dozen soldiers took up the rear. There was no sign of Talis.

On the opposite side of Hafryn, the panther shifter tightened her grip on her blade, eyes murderous.

They waited in tense silence for the Roldaerians to draw near.

Danil heard the murmur of voices and a strange, repetitive clink of metal striking stone. It seemed to come from behind them in the forest beyond the ruined building.

Hafryn heard it too. Frowning, he pointed. Two shifters dashed across the dirt floor to peer through the remains of what must have once been an arched window.

They ducked down immediately.

One motioned urgently to Hafryn.

The wolf padded over. Danil hesitated, then joined him. The muffled voices were louder, though he couldn't quite discern the words.

With the shifters crowding the edge of the window, Danil settled on his belly to peer through a small crack. A sea of epiphytes and elkhorn marred much of his view, but between the greenery he made out a broad strip of moss-covered cobblestones and the remnants of more structures.

Danil counted six men with shovels at work beside a little stream that burbled across the cobbles. A pile of dirt marked the side of a trench that ran directly beside the stream. Their shovels made harsh thuds each time they struck against stone.

A seventh man watched them work, his pale blue tabard a stark contrast against the lichen-stained ruins.

Danil held his breath in grim realization.

Magus Brianna's soldiers had already reached Altonas.

With Ronan drawing close, Danil and his companions stood trapped between the two Roldaerian forces.

13

U naware of their observers, Magus Brianna's soldiers continued to dig beside the stream. A pair picked through the dirt and inspected pebbles and jagged bits of stone before tossing them into the stream.

With consternation, Danil realized they must be searching for kiandrite. He wondered how these soldiers could tear up part of the citadel with no shifters nearby to stop them.

Crouched beside him, Hafryn glanced skyward through the window. The heavy canopy showed glimpses of dark clouds scudding low between the mountains peaks. Danil thought he saw a bird riding the thermals before it was lost in the clouds.

Blutark hissed softly and adjusted his crossbow.

The sound of soldiers crashing through the underbrush grew loud. Elania transformed into a snow leopard, her golden eyes reflecting in the shadowy light as she edged close to the large section of missing wall.

Hafryn urgently motioned for everyone to hide.

The underbrush rustled as the first of Ronan's soldiers

tracked past the building. She stared straight ahead, eyes set on some distant point. More quickly followed. To Danil's alarm, they reached the corner of the building and turned toward their digging compatriots as if drawn to them.

From his hiding point, Danil watched as Magus Ronan and his force filtered onto the street where the soldiers continued to dig. The leader straightened and gave the mage a nervous salute.

Reaching the stream, Magus Ronan turned about in a slow circle, annoyance clear on his disfigured face. He questioned the leader, his words unintelligible through the wall. His expression darkened when the man shook his head.

Blue eyes murderous, the mage waved sharply at his troops to spread out, then yelled orders at the milling diggers. The soldiers threw down their shovels and quickly fanned out into the surrounding bushes.

Magus Ronan remained near the stream. He pulled a small ball of polished onyx from his pouch and spoke crisply into it.

Hafryn swore under his breath and Danil watched in dread as three soldiers approached the very building they hid in.

A bitter coldness swept across Danil's spine. By habit, he glanced up but saw no mist form. A vision of Magus Brianna in the inn's kitchen came to him. She stared down into the bowl and muttered into a matching onyx ball.

He tugged Hafryn's sleeve in alarm but it was too late.

Ronan's gaze snapped about to stare at the wall they hunkered behind. He pointed and bellowed an order.

Hafryn pushed away from the window and yelled a warning.

The first soldier charged through the missing section of

wall. Elania was on him in a heartbeat, powerful claws raking down his back. He fell with a scream.

Blutark shot the second soldier to enter, and the third one fell after being entangled with the body. Two of Ronan's troop stepped in, their faces expressionless. Another clambered through the ruined window. All were met with roaring ferocity as shifters moved to intercept.

Danil found himself hustled to the center, the shifters forming a ring about him.

"More come!" someone shouted.

The crash and clang of fighting filled the ruins as more soldiers boiled in. Danil drew his dagger, blood thundering in his ears. He ducked in, finding a gap in the wall of Amasians to stab a soldier in the thigh. The man soundlessly fell back, to be finished off by Blutark.

Magus Ronan stepped through the broken section of wall. Blue eyes glittered as Danil met his gaze over Elania's shoulder. The snow leopard growled deep in her lungs. A glyph lit up along her spine as she roared. A solid wall of air surged toward the mage. He flung it against the stonework, creating an explosion of mud and splintered rock.

More soldiers entered, and with a coil of terror in his guts, Danil knew they would be overrun. The shifters gathered close as they were surrounded.

Ronan slowly unfurled his firewhip. It slithered on the ground like a living thing. "Give over the deadland rat," he purred. "And you all may live."

Nothing in his eyes indicated he meant it.

Hafryn's lip curled in a wolfish snarl. "You think you can enter Amas without consequences?"

The mage appeared amused by the exchange. "I assure you, everything is exactly as planned."

Suddenly, a crow dropped down through the absent

ceiling. The bird transformed mid-flight into a black haired, black-cloaked woman with twin blades. She landed on a soldier's chest and drove both blades clean through his body. She somersaulted off him as he fell, slashing another soldier across the throat and abdomen.

More crows winged inside, transforming into fearsome warriors until there was a sea of black. They seethed over the Roldaerian soldiers, cutting and slashing. Hafryn and the rest of the party joined the fray with shouts of triumph. Magus Ronan staggered back as the soldiers around him were cut down.

"Ha!" Hafryn said, driving his sword for the mage's throat.

Green light coalesced moments before Ronan transported out.

The final Roldaerian soldiers fell under a flurry of swords, claws and talons.

A quiet settled over the battle before Hafryn motioned for the injured to be checked over. A few shifters bore slashes and blade cuts. Blood left dark stains on the soil.

Sheathing his dagger, Danil put his hands on his thighs and drew in a few shaky gulps. That was closer than he liked.

The crow shifter who had entered first cleaned her swords on a soldier's pale cloak. "Apologies for our tardiness," she said as she straightened, her accent lilting. "It's not our way to make a dramatic entrance."

Hafryn gave her a crooked grin. "Your timing is impeccable."

She pressed a fist to her heart and bowed. "I'm Commander Patril of the Southlands. We patrol this quarter of Altonas."

Hafryn made hasty introductions. Patril ran a curious

gaze over Danil but said nothing. "How many patrols are in Altonas now?" the wolf asked.

"We number close to two hundred," Patril said. "Enough to take on the Roldaerians, but more of them arrive each day. We judge as many as three hundred are spread throughout the citadel."

"So many," Elania exclaimed, startled.

Patril ran an assessing gaze over them. "Let's get you to our base. You all look in need of rest and care."

She indicated they follow her out of the ruin. Other crow shifters stood guard along the street, while a couple set about putting the trench to rights. They put the cobbles back in place with care.

Danil hesitated, glancing at Hafryn. "Is it wise to go to the base? Brianna's farseeking—"

"We're aware of your particular situation, human," Patril said. She inclined her head, glossy black hair sweeping forward. "I assure you, we are prepared for it."

14

Patril and her squadron of crows escorted them deep into Altonas. All about were broken columns, the remnants of homes and palatial buildings, and moss-covered stairs leading to great platforms. Much had been reclaimed by the forest, the thick canopy casting variegated sunlight across the stone. A burbling river wended its way amidst the broken citadel. They crossed the river using a crumbling stone bridge newly patched with wooden planks.

All about were signs of Roldaerian dig sites. To Danil's eyes, they seemed haphazard and aimless, found amidst alleys, under felled trees and once in what was perhaps a cookhouse or smithy, judging by the array of hearthstones still blackened despite centuries of disuse.

"The Roldaerians arrived two days ago," Patril said, leading them down into a gully where a paved landing stretched out over a rambling stream. Danil imagined shifters had once sat on the landing's edge and sank their feet into the clear depths on warm summer nights.

"They started their mining almost immediately," Patril

added. "We've attacked many parties, yet their excavations have continued unabated."

Elania stepped over a mound of disturbed rock and soil. "There are places on the borderlands with better kiandrite yields than Altonas," she said.

Patril nodded. "And yet here they are."

Frowning in thought, Hafryn said, "I'd like a map of every dig site your patrols have come across."

The crow shifter inclined her head. "Of course."

After a time, they stepped into a courtyard stripped clean of undergrowth. Instead, a veritable collection of barrels, crates and tables stretched across the flagstones. A sizeable contingent of Amasians sat together to share a meal, while at an armory others worked on blades, arrows and metal talons. Danil saw one shifter polishing a helm suitable for a large feline.

On the far side of the courtyard was an intact tower, its yellow stone stripped of most of the lichen and moss so that it gleamed in the sunlight. Danil could see guards patrolling its heights.

Patril took them to an outbuilding on the opposite side of the courtyard. A sheltered corridor led them into what looked to be a greenhouse of hanging plants. It held an gathering of waxy-leafed orchids, elkhorn and bearded moss that hung down in massive clumps. The air felt strangely charged as a breeze swept through. Danil brushed against a flowering ginger and felt his skin tingle.

"Our healers' favorite collection of curatives," Patril said, pausing to look up at a clump of purple-lined moss. She rested her hands on her hips. "A handful of these plants have a habit of disrupting the reliability of enchantments." She smiled slightly. "I figure this would be a suitable place for you all to rest."

Hafryn turned about on his heel to study the plants. "I recognize a few." He tapped a glossy leaf no larger than his thumbnail. "This one here was banned from my clan's gathering hall after one too many pranks went awry."

Blutark muttered under his breath something about pranksters and wolves.

Ignoring his companion, Hafryn said, "We'll need enchanters on hand. I admit we underestimated the magi's fixation on Danil."

"I'll have them stationed outside," Patril promised. "A farseeking may still be possible, but the mage shouldn't be able to pinpoint your location." She indicated with her chin. "There are healing pools in the adjoining rooms. I'll have fresh towels, clothing and refreshments brought in."

Hafryn murmured his thanks and saw Patril to the doorway. They spoke quietly for a few minutes before the crow shifter departed.

Danil waited for Hafryn to return before he asked hopefully, "Are we really safe here?"

"After a fashion," the wolf allowed. He motioned for everyone to make for the healing pools. "With all of this running around, we've forgotten that the magi's hunt is a good thing."

"How do you figure that?" Danil folded his arms.

"The magi don't have what they desire," Blutark muttered as he brushed past to join Elania.

Danil met Hafryn's eyes and froze.

The wolf nodded, his gaze penetrating. "In each attack, you've been the magi's goal. And not, I believe, out of petty vengeance. They believe you are key," he said.

The deadlands.

It always came back to that. Danil was the only one in Farin who walked it. While the magi could bring a deadland walker from Scara, they'd be unfamiliar with the local terrain.

He said as much to Hafryn.

"Perhaps the magi arrived at the village thinking they could find it without help," the wolf mused.

"Most of the soldiers never got past the first scree field," Danil replied, remembering his desperate escape.

"Well, then."

Danil sighed in frustration. "I don't know what they're looking for."

"Let's hope they never force you to find out."

15

"Danil."

A hand gripped his shoulder and gently shook. "Come, wake up, *fala*."

Danil rolled onto his back and blinked blearily at Hafryn from under his nook of hanging ferns. The sun beamed high over the wolf's shoulder, bringing fiery highlights to Hafryn's braid.

"It's morning?" he mumbled.

Hafryn grinned. "Afternoon. You've slept most of the day."

Danil scrubbed his face. The muscles in his arms, shoulders and legs made themselves known. Even his belly hurt. "Gods, I ache," he grumbled.

"You and me both. Join us for a meal, *fala*."

Pushing himself up, Danil saw a handful of cushions spread out in front of platters of fruits, meat, bread and cheeses. A fire crackled merrily a short distance away, breaking the lingering coldness in the air.

Danil's belly rumbled.

With an effort, he settled on an embroidered cushion

and stretched his boots toward the small brazier. He noticed Elania and Blutark kneeling before a moss-covered marker at the far end of the greenhouse.

He hadn't seen the marker during their arrival yesterday, but now Danil watched as the glyph at the center of the marker glittered with changing light. Its swirled pattern reminded him of two ropes intertwined.

Blutark murmured something, and a softly glowing symbol made of spirals floated above his upheld palm. It joined Elania's glyph of tightly-woven lines. The two glyphs melded together before wheeling down to the ground at the foot of the marker. The co-joined glyphs winked from sight.

With a heartfelt groan, Hafryn sat down on the cushion beside Danil. His green eyes watched the pair fondly. "This place is one of the *aife*," he said. "It's a sacred place where two leylines cross."

Danil watched as Elania and Blutark created another series of glyphs. "What are they doing?"

"Honoring the leylines, so that we don't take their kiandrite gift for granted."

The white stone underneath the moss appeared brighter as the second glyph disappeared into the soil.

Hafryn pressed a fist to his heart and bowed toward the marker. "As enchanters, our two friends are particularly bound, and so they offer the twin glyph of strength and fidelity, and another of duty and consequence."

The glyph showed a mass of color, first red and yellow, before settling into a series of darker, verdant hues.

Hafryn's mouth tilted upwards. "Of course, all of Amas honor the leylines. The solstice festivals are rambunctious affairs—not at all like the solemn rituals of our enchanters." He shrugged. "We each give reverence in our own way."

Blutark eventually rose to his feet and offered his hand

to Elania. They navigated the low-hanging maidenhair ferns and took up the cushions on the other side of the platters of food. Bemusement showed on the large man's face. "I don't think drunkenness and multiple bedmates counts as honoring the leylines, Hafryn," Blutark said dryly before popping a grape into his mouth.

The wolf straightened. "Depends on what you're honoring." His green eyes twinkled.

Elania snorted as she helped herself to a hank of bread and slathered it with butter. The dark circles under her eyes already appeared diminished. "How a wolf of the northern reaches ever got past the gates of Corros, I'll never know."

"By having impeccable taste in companions," Hafryn said. He winked at Danil. "You should know the northern reaches are unfairly maligned, *fala*. We might have our share of cutthroats, swindlers and brigands, but if we declare you enemy, we'll come at you from the front."

"You just don't like the political maneuverings at Corros," Blutark said as he speared a slice of ham and filled his plate. "Help yourself, Danil. There's no ceremony here."

Famished, he loaded his plate with various meats, fruits and two servings of honeycake. He took his first bite with deliberate slowness. The sweet flavors burst on his tongue.

They ate in amicable silence for a time.

Swallowing a mouthful of ale, Danil eventually asked, "Have you all been to Corros?" He wondered how a human could live in a place where enchantments were both normal and unremarkable.

"It's a stuffy place," Hafryn said. "Pretty enough, if you have a liking for citadels carved into the side of a mountain. Too much tradition and formality for me, though. It's a wonder Sonnen turned out as he has."

Neither Elania or Blutark disagreed.

"Will Sonnen be king one day?" Danil asked.

"Certainly not, barring any disasters," Hafryn said, slicing into one of the cold meats. "He's the first cousin to the Queen. It's at her pleasure that he rules over Corros and its principality—that's everywhere from the deadland border to the end of the Orinic Mountains. A full week's flight, according to our hawk brethren."

"Does it include the northern reaches?"

"No." Hafryn crinkled his nose. "Sonnen and I met when I was scarcely more than a pup. Altonas is in his purview, however."

Danil could imagine what Altonas had once been like, filled with artisans and traders and riotous living. He glanced at a fountain overrun by tiny epiphytes, and a sculptured mountain cat that peered out from a thicket of ferns. The citadel seemed far larger than Danil imagined, perhaps even of a size to Roldaer's royal city of Anteran.

"I know that Altonas was ruined by Kaul, but why has no one ever rebuilt?" Danil asked.

"A few clans tried over the ages," Blutark said as he assembled meat atop a thick slice of bread. "But there's a strangeness here. Some argue that it's the remnants of Kaul. The younglings are particularly vulnerable."

"How so?"

"Some lose the ability to shift, or are fearful of kiandrite. Others refuse to go near certain parts of the citadel." The bear shifter squinted at the stone marker. "We are for the most part content to let the forest retake it."

"I thought nothing could affect your ability to transform," Danil said.

Elania shook her head. "The shift comes upon us when we're quite young and don't know ourselves. Shifting into our Trueforms requires strength of mind that youngsters have yet to develop."

"So some people may never learn to do it," Danil surmised.

"Oh, it's a natural part of ourselves," she replied. "But like walking, it doesn't come easily at first. There are clans for whom the first shift is a sacred occasion, for it reveals who you truly are."

"I don't get it."

Hafryn chuckled. "Our Trueforms are our spirits made flesh—inheritance has little to do with it. Take Blutark for example, whose parents are an osprey and a wren, yet he is a bear of a man in all respects." The wolf grinned when Blutark made no indication he was listening, instead concentrating on demolishing his construction of meat and bread. "It makes for interesting family gatherings."

Danil looked at the bear shifter in awe.

"Of course, some Trueforms are more common than others," Hafryn continued. "The High Reaches has an abundance of wolves and various birds of prey. The lowlands have small folk best suited to traversing the border undetected. Regardless, your Trueform is largely unknown until the first shift, although some have an inkling."

"Did you know you were a wolf?"

Hafryn tilted his head in thought. "There were indications. Games and pranks I used to play on my clanmates."

"Trickster wolf," Elania muttered under her breath.

Hafryn grinned. "I was an errant child," he conceded.

"Your childhoods are so different to mine," Danil said with yearning. If he hadn't been scavenging in the tunnels, he'd busily made himself least in sight. "Winter was always the best season—even if we had little to eat, at least there were no magi in the village. We could play without fear of disturbing them."

The three shifters looked at him with varying levels of concern and pity.

Danil straightened. "It wasn't all bad. My parents loved me deeply."

"Did the magi force them to leave with the rest of the village?" Elania asked.

He shook his head. "My pa died of the wasting sickness a few winters ago. Ma went out into the deadlands one day and never returned." He forced a shrug. "It's the way of most folk who walk the deadlands."

The shifters observed him in solemn contemplation. Danil fought the urge to shift on his cushion.

Hafryn cleared his throat. "Well, I'm glad you're no longer walking the deadlands, *fala*. Even if the circumstances aren't ideal."

Danil smiled faintly. "Has much happened here? I didn't expect to sleep so long," he admitted.

"Little enough, all things considered," Hafryn said. "Patril's crows scour the ruins, but there's plenty of hiding places. Magus Ronan is staying out of sight for now."

Danil glanced at Elania and Blutark. The enchanters made a show of appearing unconcerned, but Danil noted the lines about their eyes. "Could I farseek Ronan the way I do Magus Brianna?"

Blutark quirked an eyebrow at him, surprised. "In light of your latent abilities, it would be most difficult to attempt it on anyone other than Magus Brianna. The chances of being discovered are high."

"But you could teach me?" he pressed.

The bear looked curious. "Amasian enchanters can't perform farseekings, but the inner paths necessary to create enchantments is the same for humans and Amasians. It's possible to teach you how to quiet your mind."

Danil sat back in contemplation.

Hafryn frowned. "I know what you're thinking, Danil, and I don't like it."

Blutark didn't seem so quick to dismiss the idea. "We would benefit from Magus Ronan's capture, wolf. I for one prefer to hunt than be harried in my own lands."

Hafryn glowered at his friend.

"I'm with Hafryn on this," Elania said with a shake of her head. "If Magus Ronan discovers you, Danil, he may trap you within the enchantment. We'll have no way of freeing you."

It was a risk he was willing to take if it meant capturing the mage.

Hafryn's scowl deepened. "Besides, wouldn't Danil need a personal item of the mage's to perform the farseeking?" he asked Elania and Blutark.

The snow leopard nodded.

Danil folded his arms. "There's the talon sheaths that cut up Ronan's face."

Elania looked startled. "There is..." she allowed. "Blood holds the most potent magic."

"No."

Danil scowled at Hafryn.

"We've underestimated the magi enough," Hafryn said. "It's only by chance we have a modicum of safety now."

"But we still don't know what they're are up to," Danil argued. "If there's a chance to find out, we should take it."

Hafryn opened his mouth to argue.

"His thinking is sound, Hafryn, as is his courage," Blutark said. "You wouldn't attempt to sway an Amasian from such a gamble," he added, chiding gently.

The wolf swore under his breath. He glanced guiltily at Danil. "I don't doubt your courage or resolve, *fala*. But whatever their plan, the magi need you, too. Putting you at risk seems unwise."

Danil opened his mouth to protest.

"But—" Hafryn raised his hand. "So, too, is sitting around with our thumbs up our asses." He glanced at Blutark. "If you think it's doable, then we should try."

"Elania and I will draw up protective wards," Blutark promised.

Hafryn didn't look particularly happy, but he nodded his approval.

"Very well," Elania said, setting aside her plate. "Let's get started."

~

BLUTARK SCRATCHED out a clear space in the dirt beneath the elkhorn and motioned for Danil to stand in the center. "This is how we teach our younglings," he said.

Danil watched with trepidation as Elania inscribed a set of lines in a circle about him. Blutark joined her, scrawling more symbols into the ground. A faint hum filled the air, and then a single, large glyph made of spikes and whorls came into being. It slowly rotated in front of Danil.

Hafryn watched silently, arms folded and green eyes hooded.

Blutark settled before him.

"What do I do?" Danil asked.

"Concentrate on the glyph," Blutark commanded.

It wasn't as much guidance as he'd hoped. The glyph glowed with flecks of yellow and silver. Danil followed one fleck with his eyes. It drifted like a leaf travelling along the surface of a stream, ducking and weaving in a current. The fleck brightened. For a moment, Danil heard a remote sound that reminded him of wind rushing through deadland tunnels.

Then it was gone. The fleck fizzled out.

Danil blinked.

Elania tilted her head. "Something happened."

Danil shrugged helplessly, feeling a little foolish. "I don't think so." An obscure sound wasn't going to somehow lead him to farseeking Magus Ronan.

"Again, Danil," Blutark ordered.

With a slow breath, he picked out another fleck of slivery-yellow light. This one wheeled between the curves and sharp edges of the glyph itself. Its lazy path brought only quiet. He watched, scarcely daring to blink, until his eyes burned. It faded like the first, and so Danil picked out a new fleck.

An interminable amount of time passed as he chased flecks with his eyes.

Eventually, the glyph itself lost form and dissolved.

Danil slowly returned to himself. He startled to see the sky tinged with pink, the first evening stars already brightening. Hafryn sat with Blutark outside the circle, the wolf with his sword and whetstone. He sharpened the blade with practiced efficiency under the glow of a magelight.

"Any luck?" the wolf asked.

Danil mutely shook his head.

"Few succeed when first learning to ride the glyphs," Blutark said. He waved his hand and the circle broke apart in a small puff of dust. "We'll try again soon. But you must learn to quieten your mind."

Danil nodded, disappointment a knot in this throat.

16

The following morning, Hafryn judged it safe for Danil to leave the hanging gardens for a time. New shifters had arrived at dawn, with Danil waking to the animal sounds of snarls, roars and ear-piercing shrieks. Blutark had gone out to join them, his bear Trueform unleashing a roar that made Danil's skin pebble.

"War cries," Hafryn said, green eyes dancing. "To let our enemies know we are coming for them."

Danil imagined it enough to turn a soldier's bowels to liquid. The cacophony swelled about them, echoing off the walls of the hanging gardens.

After the morning meal, they headed out to the courtyard. Elania proposed they try an alternative setting than the hanging gardens for Danil's training, wondering if perhaps the strange herbs and succulents affected his ability to focus on the glyph.

A cool breeze sent leaves and detritus skipping across the pale flagstones. Elania marked out a spot in a relatively quiet corner, away from the gathering places and workstations. Curious looks met them, and Danil felt particularly exposed.

"Concentrate, Danil," Elania said as she brought the training glyph into being.

With a slow breath, Danil settled his attention on the slowly spinning glyph. The flecks appeared more vivid and solid in the daylight.

An unusual level of activity drew him out sometime later. The sun had scarcely moved more than a handspan. Elania extinguished the glyph with a distracted wave, her attention skyward.

A pair of eagles swooped down and transformed into two women. They joined a group of around thirty shifters gathered near the archway leading out into the ruins. A sense of urgency filled the air as another party emerged from an outbuilding, all heavily loaded with weapons.

Danil and Elania hurried across to where Hafryn stood in conversation with the crow commander.

"Has something happened?" Elania asked.

"There's been sightings of a mage in the old merchant quarter," Patril said. She handed a missive to a shifter standing behind her. The man shimmered into a sparrow and took flight, the parchment gripped in his clawed feet.

"Is it Magus Ronan?" Danil asked.

Patril shook her head. "A woman, dark hair with a white streak down the middle."

"*Brianna?*" Danil gaped. He turned to Hafryn. "She was still in Farin in my last vision."

"You've missed more than a full day, Danil, what with sleep and training and being hidden from her prying eyes," the wolf pointed out. "Easy enough for the magus to transport herself into Altonas unnoticed."

Movement caught Danil's eye as another figure stepped out of the armory. The young man looked vaguely familiar, with wavy dark hair and a pointed chin. Strangely, he wore a leather jerkin similar to Danil's, along with matching breeches.

Their eyes met, and the young man politely inclined his head before joining another party of shifters.

Danil started. "He looks like—"

"You?" Patril signaled the party. The young man pulled up the hood of his cloak as the shifters filed out of the courtyard. "It's a fair approximation. He should prove sufficient to draw the Roldaerians out."

Hafryn wrinkled his nose. "I prefer your eyes, *fala*. Such a pretty grey. Like the moon on solstice night."

Danil bit the inside of his cheek.

"Indeed," Patril said. She studied them both with a new light.

"When are we heading out as well?" Danil asked.

Hafryn grimaced. "I was hoping you'd opt to stay in the hanging gardens."

Danil gave him a flat look. "I'm more likely to draw either Magus Brianna or Ronan into a trap than anyone else."

"Agreed," Hafryn said, surprising Danil. "There's nothing I want more than to see that smug bastard Ronan's face when his schemes all tumble about him, but if things go wrong—" He shook his head. "We still have little inkling as to why they seek you."

Danil recalled how unfazed Ronan had been in their last fight. Whatever his plan with Magus Brianna, they had long moved past the distraction of losing the journal. The mage had seemed almost smug.

"If we don't stop them," Danil said. "I think something

terrible will happen. Something worse than war between our kingdoms."

Patril winged a dark eyebrow, willing to wait out Hafryn's response.

The wolf scrubbed his face. "Patril, have you a squadron of crows to accompany us?"

"I do."

Danil looked at him in hope.

"Myself, Elania and Blutark will join Danil on the ground, but I want the crows out of sight and ready the moment we draw either mage out."

The commander saluted and stepped away.

Elania cleared her throat. "If there's an opportunity, Blutark and I will continue Danil's training. I prefer that we capture both mages."

Hafryn nodded. "The sooner we cleanse Altonas, the better."

THEY SET out later that afternoon, following the path of a little stream. Hafryn consulted a rolled up scrap of parchment as he led them past spring-fed pools and cascades that wended their way between the remnants of squat buildings and interconnected structures whose former uses were beyond Danil's ability to imagine. The citadel must have once been home to thousands of shifters.

Ducking under a blossoming vine, Danil stumbled on freshly turned earth. The undergrowth was stripped bare, with detritus strewn about and a trench cutting deep into the banks of a small pool. Tiny specks of kiandrite glittered in variegated colors in the dark soil.

Hafryn crouched beside the trench and pulled out his

parchment. He scratched a marking onto it, eyebrows quizzical.

A large crystal almost fully buried in the mud caught Danil's attention. Digging it free, he wiped off the dirt, marveling at the barrel-like shape of the kiandrite crystal. It warmed in his palm.

"This is a small leyline," Blutark muttered, looking about at the trees that grew thick and high around the pool. "Scarcely worth the effort for such a poor kiandrite yield."

Danil had grown up on tales of mages battling to the death over pebbles of kiandrite. The crystal in his hand was priceless. It was astonishing that soldiers had missed it.

Elania eyed the destruction with dismay. "The larger leylines are more heavily patrolled," she murmured. "At least Danil found the lodestone."

He glanced up in surprise, unfamiliar with the term.

Blutark walked over to set his large hand over Danil's as if to feel the energy of the crystal. "A lodestone forms when a leyline intersects a place of high natural energy, like this pool," he said. "It's most unusual for a human to find one."

"You make it sound like lodestones purposefully hide from humans," Danil said with a chuckle.

Blutark didn't argue against it. The changing colors of the crystal streamed up between his fingers to reflect across his face.

Elania stepped closer as if drawn to the lodestone as well.

Hafryn swept some dirt off the parchment. "It looks like the soldiers have concentrated their digging around lodestones." He tapped a lower part of the parchment. "There's a few trenches that make little sense, but for the most part we should be able to predict where they'll hit next."

"Perhaps we should make ourselves known at such a place," Blutark muttered. "The combined draw of the lodestone and Danil might prove too tempting for the two mages to pass up."

Hafryn nodded and gazed up into the lush branches overhead. "Let Patril know, eh?" he called out.

With a flap of black wings, a crow took flight. Danil hadn't even noticed they had company.

He glanced again at the lodestone. It emitted a strange, whispery hum. "Did Kaul use lodestones in his experiments?"

Blutark stepped back to allow Elania access to the crystal. "He did."

Elania's eyes seemed to brighten as she thumbed the lodestone. "He would drain their energy into glass orbs to use as he willed." She glanced up. "If Kaul wrote of orbs in the journal, Magus Brianna might know how to do it."

Danil thought of the conversation he'd overhead so many days prior, and how eager Brianna had been to reach Altonas. "There's a big lodestone somewhere in Altonas, isn't there?"

Blutark shook his head. "Kaul drained it centuries ago."

Then why was Brianna so set on the citadel? She'd looked enlivened when she spoke of it in Farin.

Hafryn appeared to share a similar thought. "We're missing something," he muttered.

"The goal might not entirely be the acquisition of kiandrite," Blutark said in agreement.

Elania transformed into her leopard form and padded to the far side of the pool. Her head tilted up as if scenting the air. She shimmered back. "The soldiers are still close."

Hafryn consulted his map. "There's a waterfall overlapping this leyline only half a mile from here. We might be able to get ahead of the soldiers and see what they're about."

The wolf motioned for them to head out. A pair of crows dropped out of the branches to wing between the trees. There had to be at least another dozen crows overhead, but they stayed out of sight.

Before following, Danil approached the pool and dropped the lodestone into the clear water. It flashed pink and blue and sank into the depths.

Blutark clapped his shoulder in approval.

Their boots made little sound on the leaf-littered forest floor. A lichen-stained sculpture of an otter sat perched on a rock beside the stream. Scuff marks on slime marked where the soldiers had crossed to the other bank.

They followed the trail. New ruins rose up amidst the trees and undergrowth. Voices echoed in the shadows, muffled by the rush of tumbling water.

Hafryn waved at them to stay low.

Danil eased through the straggly branches of a flowering bush, careful of his steps amidst the twigs. Elania was once again a snow leopard, her dappled coat blending as she stalked between two crumbling pillars of stone.

Snippets of conversation drifted between the trees. Danil recognized the Roldaerian borderland brogue, startled by its strangeness after having spent so much time with Amasians.

Peering cautiously around the edge of a crumbling platform, he spied two soldiers standing a little apart from their companions who were already at work pulling up stained flagstones beside a small cataract. The plunging water muffled the sound of the flagstones being flung into the stream below the waterfall.

"Lieutenant's gonna pay with her flesh if we don't give Blondie something pretty," one of the soldiers muttered.

His companion made a warding sign. "Don't call him that!"

"What—Blondie?" The soldier snorted. "No mage is going to bother spying on us folk. Besides, Blondie's still fuming over losing the traitor."

Danil grew still. A thundering filled his ears. They had to be talking about him.

He hadn't given much thought to how his own people would view his actions. But stealing from a mage and giving it to their sworn enemy—it was indeed traitorous.

"Do you *want* to feed Magus Ronan's whip?" the second soldier hissed. He looked ready to back away from his companion. "Don't speak ill of the magi."

"Indeed, not," a newcomer muttered, stepping out from a path between the trees. The man pulled back his hood to reveal grey hair and a comely face lined with age.

The two soldiers hastily bowed.

"Magus," the second soldier effused, bowing deeper.

Danil threw Hafryn an alarmed look. When had this newcomer arrived in Altonas? Surely if Patril and her squadrons had known, they would have given warning.

"You're lax in your duties," the mage observed, expression severe. "Expect Magus Brianna to hear of your carelessness and disregard."

Both soldiers stiffened.

"Yes, magus."

"At your service, magus."

The mage gestured sharply. "Get to work. I wish to understand why you have all so gravely failed us in attaining our mage-crystals. I fear I have already seen enough."

The soldiers grimaced but hurried to join their

companions still busily clearing a space beside the short waterfall.

Under the mage's glare, a frenetic energy infused all of the soldiers as they set about digging a wide trench. A mound of dirt quickly grew beside the trench but no telling flash of kiandrite caught Danil's eye.

Hafryn gave Danil's boot a shake and motioned for him to back away.

Edging behind the platform, Danil followed the wolf as they quickly traipsed back the way they'd come. Elania's tail twitched back and forth in agitation as she scampered ahead, while Blutark silently took up the rear.

After a safe distance, Danil hissed, "Why are we just leaving them to steal kiandrite?"

"Because we don't know what the mage is capable of," Hafryn muttered. "I thought we'd have only Ronan or Brianna to deal with."

"Did you recognize the mage, Danil?" Blutark asked.

Now that he thought of it, Danil realized he didn't. "He's never been with Brianna during a farseeking."

Hafryn cursed under his breath. "We need Patril to send warning to the other patrols. There may be more even mages in Altonas."

17

They traced their way back via the stream as afternoon cast the trees into new shadows. The forest seemed to close in as they navigated through a maze of worn stone blocks and the wreckage of former buildings.

Danil worried about the new mage. Along with Magus Brianna and Ronan, it meant that at least four other magi were involved. He'd never heard of so many magi working together, except during the king's Name Day festivals. It smacked of something far larger than a couple of mages gone rogue against their king.

Hafryn suddenly raised his hand.

Without looking behind, he motioned for everyone to back up into a heavily overgrown ditch beside what was once a cobbled road.

Danil sank onto his belly, damp soaking through his tunic. He nervously waited, feeling exposed despite the covering foliage.

Magus Brianna stepped into view at the far end of the road. Danil's skin chilled. A magelight floated above her, casting her face in a sickly glow. No soldiers or other magi escorted her. Her cloak swept wide as mist gathered about her slippered feet. Pausing, she stood with her hands on her hips as she peered up at the remains of a collapsed wall.

Hafryn made a three-fingered signal at Blutark. The bear shifter quietly strung his crossbow with infinitesimal slowness.

Unaware, Magus Brianna uttered a series of exotic words. A strange seam of inky blackness formed beside her. Reaching within, Brianna pulled out a familiar silver bowl. She set it on a slab of stone and poured a glittering liquid from a waterskin on her pouch. Leaning over the bowl, she began to mutter an incantation.

Danil turned to Hafryn in alarm and braced for the icy bite of magic upon his skin. Blutark took aim.

"Wait," Hafryn whispered.

The bear shifter stilled.

Heart loud in his ears, Danil realized the familiar, chilling sensation had yet to sweep over him. He waited as Magus Brianna stared into the bowl and smiled. She glanced about, seeming to take measure of her surroundings. Upending the bowl, she wiped it dry with the edge of her cloak before magicking it out of sight through the black portal. She stepped off the cobbled road and strode with purpose toward a grove of trees and broken columns. The glow of the magelight faded soon after she disappeared from view.

Blutark turned to Hafryn with a scowl. "What was that about?" he hissed. "She was easy pickings."

"We should follow her," Hafryn said as he climbed the ditch.

"*What?*" Blutark spat.

"She did a farseeking," Danil said as the wolf loped ahead. "But it wasn't for me."

Muttering a curse, Blutark checked his crossbow. "I grow weary of not knowing the magi's plans." The bear shifter stalked after Hafryn.

Filled with foreboding, Danil and Elania hurried to stay apace.

∿

A THICK MIST rolled in as they trailed after Magus Brianna. It cast a gloom over the trees, ferns and low-hanging vines. Condensation made moss-covered stones gleam wetly in the cloudy dark, and set red flowers to gleaming.

Hafryn strode a few paces ahead, hand on the hilt of his sword.

"Careful. This mist is unnatural," Blutark muttered quietly in warning. He thumbed his crossbow. This close, Danil could see miniscule glyphs stir under his touch. "And we've lost our crow sentries."

Danil checked the darkened canopy in alarm. The mist was too thick to see beyond the lowest branches.

A scant mile ahead, a faint glow marked Magus Brianna's magelight.

They ducked into the underbrush when they caught sight of her. The mage crouched over the silver bowl once again, stirring its contents. Mist roiled about her, partially obscuring her work.

"She's farseeking again," Elania whispered, frowning as she peered through the foliage. "Danil?"

He sensed nothing and shook his head.

They watched as Magus Brianna finished the enchantment and continued deeper into the mist.

"Whoever it is, she has a solid bead on them," Elania murmured. She clambered to her feet, looking about at the dripping trees. "How odd, though, that whoever she's following seems to be walking along a leyline."

Hafryn's gaze snapped to her. "Are you certain?"

"It should be on your map," she said. "There's a weak leyline that runs through this area."

The wolf quickly unrolled the parchment and spread it out on a bed of mist-dampened clover. He tapped a scrawled line, frowning. "Why would anyone want to draw a mage's attention to a leyline?"

"Perhaps in the hopes of distracting the magus," Blutark suggested.

Danil studied the map, noting the various dig sites marked throughout Altonas. The trenches had started off fairly spread out, but then gradually winnowed down to a small region. The party currently stood in the center of that area. "I know the soldiers have been trying to harvest kiandrite," he began. "But this looks more like a search pattern. It could be that Magus Brianna is using leylines as a reference to find something else."

Frowning, the wolf traced a finger over the map, starting from the leyline they currently straddled. His finger ended at an area that looked no different to the rest of Altonas.

Hafryn, however, leaned back with a curse. "*Karalingra*," he murmured.

"Say what now?" Danil said, glancing down again at the parchment.

"It means 'place of endings'," Blutark said. A frown showed deep on his brow.

Hafryn nodded grimly. "It's where Kaul lies buried."

18

"This is it," Blutark murmured.

Danil turned about in a slow circle. They stood in a small grove, no different to any other they'd come across since arriving in Altonas. Vine-covered columns lay toppled amidst a carpet of moss. Much of the remaining ground was covered in ivy.

"Over here," Hafryn whispered. He pulled back a layer of ivy to reveal a set of stone stairs leading down into the earth.

Stepping close, Danil eyed the inky blackness with disquiet. Patches of dirt sat on the first couple of steps. The air felt unnaturally cold. "Gods," he muttered under his breath. It was damned creepy.

Hafryn grinned humorlessly. "I'll go first." He touched a glyph engraved into the stone before stepping down.

The stairs descended into a tunnel overrun with tree roots and dead bracken. A faint light showed at the end of the tunnel. They padded towards it and peered into a stone chamber. Lit sconces filled the chamber with an orange glow.

Magus Ronan and four others stood in a wide circle at the center of the chamber, including the silver-haired mage they'd seen earlier in the afternoon. The strangers all wore pale cloaks with Brianna's insignia dyed in the center. Together with Ronan, they chanted in an obscure language.

In the middle of the magi circle stood Magus Brianna, her hand outstretched over the stone floor. The ground swelled and heaved, then turned to water. Moments later, a white fragment of what looked like bone rose out of the liquid. More rapidly followed, whirling about Magus Brianna's raised hand before melding together to form a pale ivory staff.

"Holy pestilence and corruption," Blutark whispered, face white.

The water rippled once again as a small round orb the color of congealed blood rose out of the ground. It floated onto the top of the staff and lodged into place with a loud 'snick'.

Magus Brianna gripped the staff. Immediately, the flesh of her hand blackened and charred, then hardened like polished stone. She smiled.

"Sweet gods, what is that?" Danil whispered.

"Every evil remnant of Kaul," Hafryn managed, green eyes horrified. "Made physical once more."

"We have to stop her before she settles into her new power," Blutark muttered. Hafryn and Elania nodded.

The air about Elania shimmered a heartbeat before a snow leopard launched into the air with an ear-piercing shriek. Without thinking, Danil burst into the chamber after her, catapulting for the ring of magi with Blutark and Hafryn at his heels.

They struck a solid wall of air. Danil flew across the chamber and crashed onto his back, winded. An invisible force pressed down on his limbs, pinning him. He stared helplessly up at the ceiling. Grunts close by indicated that his companions were similarly pinioned.

The shifting of fabric warned that the magi headed for him. From his periphery, he saw Magus Brianna step out of the circle, the orb atop her staff casting bloodied shadows about the chamber.

With a gasp, Danil attempted to roll away.

"Now, now, guide," Magus Brianna tutted. Her voice had a strange whispery quality he'd never noticed before. "We have a bargain to fulfil."

She raised her blackened hand, the flesh withered and hard. Icy tendrils formed along her skin. The tendrils licked out, sweeping over Danil to where Hafryn, Blutark and Elania lay.

The three were lifted off the ground and thrown against a wall with sickening thuds.

No!

Danil found himself suddenly freed. He rolled to his feet, teeth bared.

A sudden crack filled the chamber, and then Ronan's firewhip wrapped around his throat. Danil's skin burst aflame. He fell to his knees with a choked cry. Magus Ronan yanked on the firewhip and dragged Danil across the stone floor by his throat.

He came to a halt at Magus Brianna's slippers. She crouched over him, charred fingers splayed like claws.

Vision blurred, Danil flinched his face away to avoid her touch. "Don't—!"

She offered a watery chuckle. "Do you not see, Ronan, how easily our plans fall at our feet?"

"I do, Great Lady," Ronan replied. He maintained

tension on the firewhip as Danil struggled to breathe. Every gulp of air burned in his lungs.

Magus Brianna looked Danil over. For a moment, her eyes appeared milky before returning to pale blue. "You're a traitorous creature," she murmured. The staff at her side seemed to brighten, the orb a slow roiling of blood-red power. "But I find myself wanting to give you another chance. What do you say, my dear? Should I give you another chance?"

Her pale eyes turned fully opaque, like a snowstorm over the deadlands. Danil gripped the firewhip to loosen it, uncaring of how it scorched his hands. He couldn't see where Hafryn and the others lay, but the silence from that area gave him a desperate energy.

"I'd be more than happy to convince him, Great Lady," Ronan said with an oily smile.

"Not here," Magus Brianna said, rising. She stepped over Danil as if he were of little consequence. The staff made a dull boom every time it struck the floor.

"You heard her, rat," Ronan said.

Coils of red agony tightened Danil's throat. He gasped, vision momentarily blackening as he was wrenched to his feet. The firewhip cut deeper into his throat as Ronan tugged him toward the tunnel. Wetness and a hot coppery tang flooded his awareness.

Danil turned desperately toward his companions. They lay in a tangled mess on the floor, mist writhing over them.

The firewhip constricted in warning. "Move," Ronan ordered.

The magi ringed around him as they emerged on the surface. Mist sat even thicker about the trees and undergrowth.

Magus Brianna planted the bone staff into the ground

and raised her charred hand. The mist in front of her condensed into a portal latticed with blood-red veins. The first of the magi stepped through and disappeared.

Danil dug in his feet as Ronan dragged him forward.

A terrible roar suddenly filled the grove.

Something massive and golden dropped down through the canopy, disturbing the mist in a whirling gust of wind. Expansive golden wings shot with bronze unfurled, the earth vibrating as the dragon landed in a billowing cloud of moss and leaves.

Dragon Prince Sonnen had arrived.

19

Sonnen roared with such ferocity it reverberated through Danil's bones. Taloned claws raked down one mage's torso. The woman flew lifelessly into the bracken.

Another mage dived for the portal, but the silver-haired mage planted his feet. He threw a bolt of flame up at Sonnen's elongated snout. The dragon appeared wholly unaffected. Flames licked the side of his mouth.

The firewhip suddenly clenched about Danil's throat. Ronan wrenched hard, sending him off his feet. Danil flailed, blindly reaching out for the nearest bush. His fingers gouged into the bark as Ronan took a step toward the portal.

Spears of ice whipped overhead from Magus Brianna, only to be met by a wall of flame. Danil's back warmed as he scrambled for greater purchase.

Someone screamed, and from the edge of his vision Danil saw the grey-haired mage bolt for the portal, his clothing on fire.

A boot slammed down on Danil's hand. He lost his grip on the bush with a cry. Ronan dragged him closer to the portal.

Magus Brianna thumped her bone staff into the ground. The dirt trembled as the orb spat out a torrent of red-tinged ice. The shards hissed as they swept over Sonnen and struck the surrounding leaves and branches. Sonnen's golden scales deepened to bronze as he took a powerful breath and released an answering fireball.

Danil slid on his belly across the detritus as Ronan reeled in the firewhip. The portal loomed over him.

"Sonnen!" he choked out desperately.

A massive tail swept across and knocked Ronan off his feet.

The handle of the firewhip went flying, and suddenly Danil was released. He scurried back on his heels, gasping for breath as the firewhip slithered after its owner.

Sonnen raised powerful talons to strike Magus Brianna. She lifted her staff, lip curling. The dragon smashed the staff to the side, and it was only by some unknowable magic that the woman retained her grip. She sent glittering shards of ice at Sonnen, only for them to tinkle off his scales like glass.

Magus Ronan suddenly appeared at her side and grabbed her about the waist. The mage dived for the portal, taking Magus Brianna with him. Her outraged scream rang out before the portal closed behind them with a solid burst of red-tinged light.

Danil sank against the dirt. His throat hurt like fury. He didn't want to touch it for fear of discovering how deep the burn went. Everything felt raw and scorched, his chest too tight for his thundering heart.

The dragon transformed into the familiar, tall man with black hair and large shoulders. Sonnen knelt beside him, golden eyes alarmed. "Danil—"

With an effort, Danil pushed his hand aside and

staggered for the stairs leading down into the chamber. Against the far wall, Hafryn stirred, weakly lifting his head. Blutark remained as a bear, unconscious and breathing harshly. The snow leopard beside him pressed her nose into his ribs, making a distressed chuffing sound.

Sonnen swept past Danil.

"Let me see, Elania," the dragon said gently. He pressed a hand to Blutark's side. "Fear not. He will be well once the healers see to him." His hand glowed for a few heartbeats.

The leopard licked the bear's ear, smoothing the fur back. Blutark seemed to breathe easier.

Hafryn coughed weakly. Without thinking, Danil eased him to sitting, studying his face searchingly. "I'm well, *fala*," the wolf said. His freckles stood out on his pale face as he touched Danil's collarbone. "Your throat..."

Sonnen turned Danil about and placed a large palm on his neck. Danil winced at the faint hissing sound.

"As a prince of fire, I can undo the worst wrought by my element, but you will need salves to lessen the scarring," Sonnen said.

Danil scarcely cared about that. They'd just experienced a resounding defeat.

The dragon lifted one of Danil's hands, turning it palm-up. The skin appeared blistered and raw. Expression meditative, the dragon traced a whorled symbol in the air just inches above Danil's skin. A golden glyph settled on his palm. The blisters and redness faded. The dragon repeated the glyph on Danil's other hand.

Danil experimentally clenched his fists and opened them again. The skin was unmarked save for the whorled glyphs that glittered on both palms. "Thank you," he managed, voice hoarse.

Sonnen sat back, golden eyes firm. "You were reckless in

your fight, Danil of Farin. A firewhip can behead a man, if the wielder wishes it so."

He resisted the urge to touch his throat. "I couldn't let them take me through the portal."

Hafryn rested his head against the wall, eyes closed. His throat bobbed as he swallowed. "One would think you're irrelevant now." He opened on eye. "Sorry, *fala*, but it's true. Using Kaul's bones for magic makes Magus Brianna an adversary few can beat."

Sonnen's eyes narrowed. "The magus has indeed fashioned herself a staff of corruption." He swept a measuring gaze over Danil. "The fact the magi tried to take you indicates that the staff is only part of their goal."

That's what Danil feared. Magus Brianna still needed him to find something in the deadlands.

"I believe I know why, Danil of Farin."

Both Danil and Hafryn turned to look at the dragon.

Elania shimmered into her human form, her amber eyes wide. "You were able to decipher Kaul's journal," she deduced while running a hand over Blutark's brow.

Sonnen rumbled. "It took some wrangling. One of its secrets was the halfbreed's attempt to create a lodestone beneath the deadlands."

Hafryn frowned, expression tired. "Lodestones occur naturally, Sonnen. They can't be forced."

"We know that Kaul discovered how to compel Roldaerian leylines to produce kiandrite," Sonnen said. "According to his journal, he also manipulated them so that they formed into a lodestone of his making."

"Like a large crystal?" Danil wondered, thinking of the lodestone he'd found.

Sonnen nodded. "It is my belief that the lodestone still exists, buried in the remains of his workroom deep underground. And no doubt the Corrupt One believes it, also."

Hafryn's mouth quirked. "Hence why she needs Danil— she doesn't know where to look."

"Nor does Danil," Sonnen pointed out soberly.

Danil nodded, thinking. Back in Farin, Magus Brianna had mentioned glyphs at the entrance meant to drive people away. He thought of the changing terrain of the deadlands, how at times he'd been driven to navigate dangerous sinkholes and surging meltwater instead of traversing safer routes across solid rock. He'd never given much thought over such choices, but now he suspected he knew why.

He glanced up. "If you can get me some parchment, I can draw the places in the deadlands I won't go." He smiled, resolve hardening. "I can map out the entrance to Kaul's workroom."

20

Blutark regained consciousness as they carried him up out of the chamber. The bear shifter grumbled at the manhandling, with even a quelling look from Sonnen not enough to quieten him.

"Quit your huffing," Elania snapped at Blutark as she and Hafryn lowered him onto a bed of moss. "You will let me tend to you."

Blutark threw her a surprised look.

Sonnen's mouth twitched slightly. "You broke some ribs, my friend. Never fear—you'll be ready for battle soon enough." He glanced about at the mist lingering about the tree roots. "Elania, will you stay with him? I must fly Danil to Corros."

Danil turned to him in shock. "What? No!"

"It was my purpose in coming here, Danil," the dragon said, unmoved. "You can draw a map just as easily in Corros. And more safely, I might add."

"I'm not going."

Hafryn frowned. "Danil—"

"No." He glared at the shifters. "You saw Magus Brianna.

I won't go to Corros when she can follow me there while using Kaul's bones for a staff." He turned back to the dragon. "I won't go."

A considering light showed in Sonnen's eyes.

Danil forced himself to hold the measuring gaze, his jaw set.

"Very well," the dragon murmured, ignoring Hafryn's gasp of dismay. "But you will not go anywhere, not even the privy, without two enchanters as escort. Understood?"

Danil nodded quickly.

"Nor will you come with us to the deadlands."

He gaped. "But I know the deadlands better than anyone!"

"Then you'd best map it thoroughly," Sonnen rumbled.

Danil bit his lip. He'd only suggested the map as a starting place. Much of the surrounding landscape was in constant flux.

"Take what's given, *fala*," Hafryn said. "A map leading us to the lodestone is more than we could have hoped for."

Just then, Patril and a squadron of crows broke through the mist. The commander's dark hair stuck out in such a manner that Danil couldn't help but think of feathers in wild disarray. Her swords were unsheathed and bloodied. She ran a quick gaze over them before motioning for a shifter dressed in dark green to Blutark's side. The shifter pulled out a small jar of iridescent liquid from his pouch.

Sonnen rose to his feet. "What news, Commander?"

"My prince," Patril said, giving the dragon a bow. "We've seen attacks throughout Altonas. Most of the Roldaerians have been routed, but a few hold out in the old artisan quarter."

Danil watched as Elania took the iridescent jar from the newcomer and roughly dabbed a glyph onto Blutark's side.

The bear shifter gave a grumbly hiss. Elania's eyes narrowed.

Ignoring them, Sonnen said to Patril, "I have a contingent approaching from Corros." He glanced up at the tree canopy. "I flew ahead, but the first company should be here momentarily. My enchanters are among them—I suggest you hold the border around the artisan quarter until their arrival, as there may yet be more magi in hiding."

Patril inclined her head. "Yes, my prince." She hesitated when Blutark flinched under Elania's ministrations. The crow healer bent to help but froze as Elania's lip curled in warning. "My healer is adept at working on all Amasians, no matter their Trueform."

Sonnen smiled. "As is Elania."

Patril watched the snow leopard for a moment longer but wisely didn't object.

"Commander, we have need of a place where the magi cannot discover our activities," Sonnen said.

"The hanging gardens are available to you, my prince." The commander motioned for a handful of crows to step forward. "My best fighters and enchanters will escort you."

After murmuring his thanks, Sonnen turned to Elania and Blutark. "Meet us there once you've both sorted things out."

Blutark looked mildly chagrined as Elania scrawled another glyph on his skin. The snow leopard looked too furious to acknowledge Sonnen.

They left the grove, Danil taking a final glance before the mist stole his view. "Are Elania and Blutark alright?"

Hafryn snorted. "They're fine. Nothing that an honest heart-to-heart won't fix."

They took a winding path back to the main base, using a rickety wooden bridge to cross the river once again. Two crow enchanters stayed apace with Danil, even crowding out Hafryn until the wolf settled for walking a few paces in front.

Eventually they reached the sprawling courtyard with its outbuildings and watchtower. As they strode across to the building leading into the hanging gardens, a large shadow blackened the sky above them.

Danil looked up in alarm. Blue scales and wings even larger than Sonnen's dragon Trueform bore down on them.

"Ah," Sonnen said with a benign smile. "Our war enchanters from Corros have arrived."

The blue dragon landed in the courtyard in a vortex of dust and leaves. In his powerful talons he carried a large wooden box the size of a shed. The dragon carefully set it down before transforming into his human form. Danil was surprised at the sight of an unassuming, dark-haired young man with mild brown eyes and a face still rounded by the last vestiges of childhood.

The end of the wooden box opened, revealing twenty shifters. All wore mottled black and grey tunics and breeches reminiscent of those Hafryn had worn when they'd last met in the deadlands.

The blue dragon strode across the courtyard. "My prince," he said to Sonnen with a curt bow.

"Cousin," Sonnen said. "Thank you for your service."

The blue dragon straightened, mouth thin. "I assume my family's debt is paid in full."

"Not quite. There is another company awaiting transport at Corros."

The young man's jaw rippled. "Very well."

He stepped back and transformed into his blue dragon Trueform. With a powerful sweep of his massive wings, he burst back into the sky.

Danil stared, mouth agape as the dragon spiraled through low-lying cloud before wheeling towards the nearest mountain peak.

"It's a great insult for a dragon to be used as a pack mule," Hafryn explained, eyes also on the sky. "Well, it's insulting for all Amasians, but dragons are particularly sensitive."

Sonnen looked at him sidelong, unamused. Danil couldn't help but notice the flames licking across the pupils of his eyes.

Hafryn grinned.

A trio of newly arrived shifters came up to Sonnen and bowed, murmuring greetings before heading for the stone watchtower.

Hafryn watched them go before turning back to the war enchanters gathering in the courtyard. "Think we have enough fighters, Sonnen?"

"Only a few will join me in the tunnels to retrieve the lodestone," Sonnen said. "The rest will remain atop to defend the entrance." He turned to Danil. "Speaking of which, it's time we test your recollections."

Danil nodded gamely.

Sonnen took the lead as they strode down a light-filled corridor and stepped into the familiar greenhouse with its hanging gardens of bracken ferns and epiphytes. Low cloud made the air damp, but one of the crow enchanters relit the brazier to break the worst of the chill.

Hafryn sat down on a thatched mat beside Danil as another shifter brought in with a few lengths of parchment and charcoal. Sonnen settled opposite them, closer to the entry. A handful of shifters came and went, the dragon issuing soft orders in preparation for the deadland incursion.

Using Farin as the starting point, Danil traced out the deadlands. He marked out the dangerous fungi groves and escarpments and mineshafts. Winter had brought with it newly collapsed tunnels and sink holes. He noted them down, too, along with the shale and scree fields he'd walked for much of his life.

Despite his diligence, a small area of parchment remained blank. It was near the south-western edge of the deadlands about five miles from Farin, where a mountain escarpment often tumbled great yellow boulders onto the blackened rocks far below. Danil remembered waking up at night during his childhood, frightened by the thundering crash of stone in the distance.

Danil sat back, rubbing his aching hand.

Hafryn hummed in thought. "I've never patrolled those parts," the wolf said. He glanced at Sonnen, who watched Danil work with hooded eyes. "Perhaps the enchantment drives away Amasian folk, too."

"It stands to reason. Kaul preferred his human aspect, and his magi brethren more so." Sonnen leaned across to hand Danil a fresh piece of parchment. "It will be difficult, Danil, but draw any feature you can recall of the area."

Biting his lip, Danil tried to think back on the last time he'd even neared the area, realizing it had to be at least a summer ago. A sense of disquiet always kept him away from the escarpment. He idly drew it onto the map.

The only time he'd only truly entered the area had been the week his ma had gone missing. He remembered the desperation as he searched the tunnels, fighting instinct in the hope that just around the corner would be his ma, alive and well.

His focus narrowed down to a tunnel, the walls surprisingly smooth and shiny like onyx that seemed to swallow the light of his torch. Danil recalled his feet sliding on the polished ground as the urge to flee fought with the raw need to keep up the search. There'd been strange symbols on the walls, ones that glittered dark red like drying blood. But he'd pushed on until he reached a dead end in the tunnel. Danil never found her.

Blinking, he looked down at the fresh charcoal scratchings. "That's the place."

"Are you certain?" Sonnen studied the parchment. "One would need a powerful desire to reach it."

Danil nodded, swallowing. "I'm certain."

It seemed enough for the dragon. "Very well. Hafryn, when the last of the contingent arrives, be sure to vet them. You've walked the deadlands often enough to know what to look for."

"No flat-footed bison. Got it," Hafryn said with a lazy salute.

Danil wiped his stained fingers on his breeches. "Do you think Magus Brianna can get past the glyphs to Kaul's workroom? Is she powerful enough?"

The dragon hesitated. "In time, little may stop her. Right now, she clearly prefers to use your knowledge over her ability to control Kaul's remnants." He sighed. "But she'll grow powerful quickly."

Danil scrubbed his arms. "Her skin looked charred as if by fire."

"The staff and orb are cursed magic of the darkest order," Sonnen said, troubled. "With each passing moment, she becomes corruption. We haven't been so at risk since Kaul himself."

"Considering her particular bent, she may be even worse," Hafryn added, mouth pulling downwards.

"How so?" Danil asked.

"Ice," Sonnen said grimly. "The bitterness of winter, the seed left frozen underground, the heart turned cold."

Danil shuddered. "Can you stop her?" he asked Sonnen, afraid of the answer. "Her magic didn't seem to affect you."

"It helps to be impervious to almost all magicks," Hafryn said with a wry smile.

Sonnen grunted. "If the Corrupt One gains control of the lodestone—no. There will be no one to stand against her." The gold in the dragon's eyes darkened. "That's why it's vital we remove the lodestone from her grasp."

Danil slid the maps across to Sonnen. "I still think I should go with you. The area around the escarpment will have changed a lot since I last strode there."

Sonnen carefully folded the parchments and tucked them into his belt. "I have eagles already scouting the deadlands. A few sweeps over the area will give us an inkling of what we face."

"I hope it's enough," Danil murmured, trying to subdue his unease.

"It will be," Sonnen promised. "By tomorrow night, the lodestone will be ours."

21

Respite finally came that night. At the dragon's urging, Danil crawled into a quiet nook below the canopy of hanging greenery. Curled under a pile of blankets, he let the murmur of voices from the other side of the wall lull him to an exhausted sleep.

The brightness of the moon woke him a while later.

He lay on his back, unable to sleep, watching clouds scud across the stars. The sounds of folk coming and going in the courtyard outside were muted. Occasionally a winged creature spiraled overhead, and Danil wondered if it were one of the enchanters tasked with watching over him.

It was a few hours yet until dawn. By midday, he'd have to watch as the contingent flew for the deadlands without him. He could hardly bring himself to examine how he'd feel when the time came. Against all expectation, he'd made friends amongst the shifters.

Smothering a sigh, Danil rolled over. He startled to see Hafryn a scant foot away under the splayed leaves of a staghorn. The wolf shifter had rolled off his blankets in his sleep.

The muted light cast gentle shadows on Hafryn's cheekbones and the slope of his freckled nose. Danil ran his gaze down the length of the wolf's body; it was a rare opportunity to study Hafryn unawares. He was rangy like his wolf form, all long limbs and corded muscle. A tuft of red hair showed at the neck of his tunic, a dusting of freckles visible on his bare arms. His feet were bare and tangled up in his blanket.

Danil returned his study to the shifter's face, only to find Hafryn awake. Mild amusement showed in the shifter's eyes.

Cheeks hot, Danil made to roll over but Hafryn reached out. With slow cautiousness, the wolf shifter took Danil's hand and threaded their fingers together.

Unexpected heat flooded Danil's belly. Desperately grateful for whatever darkness the night afforded, he parted his mouth to speak but found no words.

Hafryn merely watched him, the moonlight pale on his eyelashes. Heart thundering, Danil watched him back.

After a time, Hafryn closed his eyes. He was asleep in moments, snoring softly.

Danil glanced at where their fingers lay still intertwined on the ground. The texture of sword callouses on Hafryn's palm brought an odd peace and comfort. He found himself unwilling to let go.

A short while later, sleep took him.

22

Hunger woke him soon after dawn.

Staggering blearily toward the campfire, he collapsed down beside Sonnen as the dragon spoke quietly with Hafryn. Both men donned the strangely mottled tunics and breeches made to blend with the deadlands.

The dragon acknowledged him by handing over a small loaf of bread.

Mumbling his thanks, Danil broke it open, fingers singed as steam wafted up. He tore the bread into three and shared the pieces before biting down. The taste of cinnamon and nuts exploded on his tongue. Danil chewed with relish.

Hafryn watched with amusement. "As I was saying, Sonnen, I know you think Gavril will be useful, but he's as light-footed as an ox. We don't want to lose anyone to a rock fall because they stomp about like drunken moose."

"What are your thoughts, Danil?" Sonnen asked.

Danil swallowed a mouthful of bread. "You might have injuries if you don't land close to the entry point." He paused, blinking. "You *are* flying everyone there, right?"

"Griff will transport our enchanters," Sonnen said.

Danil didn't recognize the name.

"He's the blue dragon," Hafryn supplied.

Danil nodded, stretching his bare toes toward the warmth of the fire. "Have the hawks returned yet from the reconnaissance? I need to update the maps before you go."

"I'll have them brought in soon," the dragon promised. His gaze sharpened. "Now, may I see your hands, Danil of Farin?"

Danil paused, startled by the turn of conversation. He carefully set down his hank of bread and obeyed.

Sonnen turned both hands palm-up. In their center was the whorled glyph the dragon had created to heal his burned skin. The twin glyphs shined golden, solid and unchanging. Danil expected them to have faded by now, their healing powers spent.

"These are the mark of my House," Sonnen said.

Danil's gaze snapped up in surprise. The dragon looked as stony-faced as ever, but his eyes softened slightly.

"They are both protection and belonging," Sonnen said. His golden eyes turned penetrating. "You have stood true to my House, defending it and those I hold dear, without prompting or personal gain. Even when I doubted you."

Danil stared.

"Know that you have a place among us, Danil." Sonnen held his gaze until he nodded. "The House of Corros will always welcome you."

His chest grew tight. He hadn't thought Sonnen even liked him. "Thank you," he murmured.

"My House glyph was earned, Danil. Not given," Sonnen said, his voice subterranean. "Never forget that."

Danil nodded again. He cleared his throat with a struggle. "I won't," he promised.

Hafryn clapped him on the shoulder. "Well done, *fala*," he congratulated, expression fond.

The dragon turned the full force of his attention onto Hafryn. "And what of you, wolf? Must I strip myself of scales before you see my House worthy of you?"

Danil glanced at Hafryn in surprise. Now that he thought of it, he couldn't recall seeing the House glyph on the wolf's body.

"Wolves of the northern reaches don't ally themselves to particular Houses," Hafryn said haughtily.

Sonnen quirked an eyebrow. "Despite all evidence to the contrary," he observed.

Hafryn sniffed.

"In time, wolf," Sonnen promised. It seemed like an old argument. He turned back to Danil. "Normally, Danil, your welcoming would be a cause for much drinking and feasting."

"Oh, aye," Hafryn said with a wide grin. "You've not yet been privy to an Amasian bacchanal, *fala*. It is a thing of wonder and delight."

"Wolves and their debauchery," Sonnen muttered under his breath.

"*Celebration*," Hafryn countered, showing his teeth. "In all its forms."

Danil felt his cheeks heat up as Hafryn's grin turned lascivious. He thought of the previous night and felt his face flame even redder.

"Alas, it must be postponed," Sonnen said. "We will honor you properly in due time, Danil. For now, the task is battle and subterfuge." His eyes glowed with flames. "And the destruction of the Corrupt One."

∾

SONNEN LEFT SOON after to discuss the mission with the war enchanters. Two crow enchanters settled in the branches overhead, almost invisible amidst the greenery. A shifter arrived with a fresh platter of fruits, cheese and spiced ale.

Hafryn took platter with a murmur of thanks, setting it down in front of Danil.

Danil glanced at the mottling of bruises on Hafryn's arms and face. He recalled the sickening crunch as the wolf had struck the chamber wall. "I'm glad you weren't badly hurt."

The wolf smiled at his concern. "That was luck," he admitted. "And stupidity."

Danil shrugged. "We didn't have much choice." A slight breeze caused the fern fronds to dip and sway above his head.

Hafryn threw him a warm look. "I think that's where you're wrong, *fala*. Sonnen was right—you've been in the thick of things from the outset. A wise man would have taken the offer of sanctuary in Corros."

Danil picked up a slice of cheese. He'd not had time to truly analyze why he'd chosen to remain at Altonas. There were truths he wasn't quite ready to explore.

"After tonight, we'll turn all attention to Magus Brianna," Hafryn added.

Danil's mouth quirked. "I don't think I'll be much use once Sonnen has the lodestone."

"Is that what you think? That you're useful only because Magus Brianna needs a guide in the deadlands?" Hafryn frowned.

Danil grimaced. "You know Magus Brianna won't sit quietly after losing the lodestone." He shook his head. "She'll want vengeance, and she can find me in a heartbeat. Anyone near me will suffer for it."

"Sonnen knows all that. He still welcomed you into his House. Then there's the matter of you being able to farsee, for all that you need training to do it at will. You've never flinched from a dangerous situation, whether it's against a mage." Hafryn's mouth quirked. "Or a shifter who's about to steal your day's work. As for Magus Brianna, I'll stand at your side, just as you've stood by mine." He ran his gaze over Danil, green eyes perplexed. "Must I explain your worth, *fala?*"

Danil felt suddenly snared by the wolf's regard. A question lay behind Hafryn's gaze, one he could answer if he was brave enough. He swallowed. "If it were reversed, and Magus Brianna was after you, would you want me at your side?"

The wolf smiled. "I think the more important question is, could I dissuade you?"

The heavy weight in Danil's throat eased. "No," he murmured.

"Well, then." Hafryn edged forward, eyes bright. "It seems we're together in all things."

Danil couldn't help but snort. "That's a bit of a stretch."

"Oh, I don't think so."

The wolf leaned close enough for Danil to feel his breath on his cheek. His eyes closed of their own volition. His skin tingled. He sensed Hafryn tilt his head, seeking. Their mouths brushed.

A throat cleared behind them.

"When you're finished."

They parted to see Blutark leaning against the entry, arms folded. Elania stood beside him, expression amused, together with a stranger bearing a symbol of outstretched wings on her tunic. There was no telling how long the trio had stood there.

"Gods cursed, cock blocking—"

"What was that, Hafryn?" Blutark said, grinning.

Hafryn smoothed down his braid. "You heard me. You're an asshole, bear."

Face burning, Danil wiped his mouth with the back of his hand.

"And you're as distracted as a pup," Blutark countered, pushing off the entry. He moved a little stiffly, arms close to his ribs.

The wolf didn't argue the point. He shrugged and said, "At least you're looking better."

Blutark eased himself down beside Hafryn, stretching his boots toward the campfire. "I'll be ready for tonight." He clasped the wolf's forearm and then turned to Danil. "I believe we have you to thank for this." He fished out the sheaf of parchment with Danil's scrawled markings of the deadlands.

"I—yes," Danil said. "It's not complete, though."

"Cala here has just returned from a reconnaissance flight," Elania said, motioning for the woman to join them. "Let's see if we can match up what she's seen with your memories."

The woman knelt beside Danil and they set to work. The landscape had changed significantly, but together they figured out a clear path to the tunnel mouth that lead down to the lodestone.

"This is good," Hafryn said, smoothing out the map. Firelight danced across the parchment.

Elania leaned over. "We'll have to play least in sight, particularly in the scree field. The Corrupt One will expect us to go after the lodestone."

Blutark glanced up through the bracken ferns. "Tonight

there should be sufficient cloud cover to block out the moon."

The air between them and the entry suddenly changed.

A cloud gathered and quickly formed into a wall of dirty, bloodied ice. It rippled.

"Back!" Hafryn said, rolling to his feet. His sword slid out of its sheath with a hiss. He gathered with Elania and Blutark before the portal. The two crows dropped down from their perches, transforming into two enchanters.

Magus Brianna stepped through. The skin of her arms appeared wrinkled and burnt, her fingers almost claw-like as she gripped the bone staff. The corruption had spread to under the sleeve of her robe. Streaks of discoloration lined her neck. The red orb atop the staff seemed to pulse like a heartbeat.

Danil met her gaze.

"Well, well," she purred, her voice like being blasted with icy needles. "My wayward guide."

Without thinking, Danil snatched up the parchment and tossed it into the fire. It caught alight with a soft puff.

Cala moved to block the mage from approaching the campfire.

Magus Brianna smirked. She raised the staff.

Hafryn tensed, a growl issuing from deep in his throat. In front of Danil, the crow enchanters wove symbols into the air.

Magus Brianna slammed the staff into the ground. A wall of ice shot out and lifted them all off their feet. Danil flew backwards in a wild tumble. He came to rest against the curved base of a fountain. He struggled to get up, winded. Ash from the deadened fire floated about him.

Magus Brianna stood before him. Danil froze as her blue

eyes momentarily flickered to white. She grabbed his arm in a punishing grip. The biting pain of ice made him cry out.

"Come, Danil," she said. "We have much to do."

She raised her hand. A portal of blood and ice solidified in front of them. She stepped through, pulling him with her.

He saw Hafryn burst through the vines, horror written on his face. Then coldness enveloped him and catapulted him away.

They burst into being above the refuse pit on the outskirts of Farin. Magus Brianna held him suspended in the air. Danil balked in her grip.

The cloying stench of rot swirled about them. Danil could see the huts marking the edge of the village.

"What are we doing here?" he gasped.

Magus Brianna smiled. Veins of white showed in her eyes. "I give you evidence that I keep my word, guide."

Suddenly released, Danil dropped onto the sandy side of the refuse pit. He toppled head over foot before striking the soggy and rancid bottom. The stench of refuse and rotting flesh made him gag. Above him, Magus Brianna laughed.

Clambering to his feet, Danil placed a hand over his mouth. Flies burst up to land on his arms and face. He flailed wildly, stumbling over a mound of something wrapped in stained cloth. The cloth burst open to reveal maggoty flesh.

Danil staggered back, gagging.

Soldiers took up position on the rim of the refuse pit. They laughed at his attempt not to vomit.

A few feet away, something glittered in the rubbish. An emerald ring. Danil thought he recognized it as Vellum's. The village healer had treasured it beyond all reason. And it was attached to—

He flailed back with a cry. A hand. The ring was attached to a hand.

Spinning about, Danil choked on his fear as he noticed the lumps of rotting flesh encased in tunics and breeches. There was the plain circlet young Callan refused to take off, lodged now upon a skull with flesh picked bare. He noticed the innkeeper's over-worn boots, the staff old Hannah used to round up her chickens.

They're all here...

Everyone from Farin. Every single villager. Even Hannah's stupid dog, lying bloated in the afternoon sunlight.

All dead. Unnoticed and unavenged.

Danil fell to his knees and screamed his anguish.

23

Time grew difficult to judge. The sun moved in increments, moving inexorably closer to the time when Sonnen would lead fighters across the deadlands. Danil's only solace was that if Magus Brianna's attention remained fixed on him, she might not realize the Amasians' plans.

Danil settled his gaze on a midpoint on the side of the pit. Tufts of dead grass dotted the refuse. He didn't want to see what lay about him now that a cloudless sky exposed the worst of it.

New soldiers arrived to replace those guarding him. Cloth covered their noses and mouths, no doubt soaked in something perfumed to block out the worst of the stench. As the afternoon stretched on, the stench grew more fetid. Flies buzzed about, and Danil heard the scurry of rodents amongst the refuse.

His one hope was that Hafryn and the others remembered enough of the destroyed map to find the entrance to Kaul's workroom. He wasn't sure how long he could hold out against the magi.

The shifters wouldn't rescue you, anyway.

The thought came unbidden and stripped him of strength. Danil put his hands on his knees, trying to take a sip of breath that didn't make his stomach recoil. The world spun.

It was true, though, wasn't it? He was just a human. He'd gotten involved of his own volition. The Amasians had no cause to come find him, not when they had everything needed to thwart Brianna and her magi cohorts.

Danil forced himself to straighten.

They arrived mid-afternoon.

Magus Ronan peered over the edge of the pit, smirking. He was wore a crisp white doublet and dark breeches. His firewhip sat coiled from his belt, its tongue white and hungry. Beside him, Magus Brianna looked resplendent in a green corset and flowing skirts. Her hair was pulled up in waves about her head, revealing her long neck with its blotchy, corruption-infused skin. She seemed unaffected by the cold, her withered arms bare to the breeze that streamed across from the deadlands.

"The rat in the rubbish pile," Ronan said, gazing down at him. His voice carried in the quiet. "How quaint."

Magus Brianna tilted her head, her smile cool. "I thought you would like it, my dear. A fair reward for his treachery."

Danil returned their gazes stonily.

The breeze brought a waft of the refuse pile up to the magi. Magus Brianna's eyes watered as she delicately covered her nose.

"Oh my," she murmured. "Perhaps it is a bit too much, wouldn't you say, Ronan? For all his faults, Danil is just an impressionable young man, poorly educated and easily waylaid."

Ronan gave a dark smile. "I fear he may waylay us as well, Great Lady."

She tilted her head, pondering. "Do you disagree, Danil?" she called down. "Your commitment to fulfil our bargain will make things much easier on you."

Danil said nothing, watching carefully.

"Do come up here, Danil," Magus Brianna said. "Don't be shy. We have much to discuss."

The soldiers along the rim of the pit raised their crossbows.

Seeing no other choice, Danil gingerly climbed the loose soil lining the side of the pit. He sucked in cleaner air at the top, feeling the tightness in his chest loosen a little.

"Please, kneel," Magus Brianna murmured as she delicately covered her nose from the stench of him.

Danil's lip curled.

The firewhip snapped out, coiling about his neck. It bit deep. Ronan yanked on the whip, and Danil lurched forward. His face hit the dirt hard, and before he could move, soldiers wrenched him onto his knees. Strong hands on his shoulders forced him in place.

"Excellent," Magus Brianna said.

Ronan released the firewhip with a negligent flick. The firewhip's tongue touched the ground and took on a faint pink tone, its hunger awakened. Danil resisted the urge to rub his throat. There'd be blood for certain.

"Now," Brianna murmured. Striations of white showed in her pupils. "Tell us about your duplicity."

Danil stared at her in confusion.

Magus Brianna gave a coy shrug. "My journal, Danil. You cannot think we've forgotten your thievery."

"A hangable offence," Ronan added with a soft tut.

"Kaul's journal was never yours to begin with!" Danil snarled.

"Ah, so you know whose writings it contains," Magus Brianna said with a pleased smile.

Danil closed his mouth in alarm.

"What else did the Amasians tell you, hmn?" she pressed.

He resolved to tell them nothing.

Ronan shook his head. "More duplicity," he tutted.

Anger flared hot in his chest. "And what was the duplicity of the people here in Farin?" he asked with a snarl. Even atop the rim, the stench was overpowering.

"Oh, they were indeed innocent folk," Brianna said. Her expression turned sympathetic. "Don't fret, Danil. The shifters will be held accountable."

No, she couldn't mean...

Magus Brianna raised her eyebrows. "For too long they have invaded our deadlands and stolen our mage-crystals. Our beloved King has charged us with setting things aright."

Danil stared at her in horror.

"King Liam is no fool, my dear Danil. He knows few Roldaerians would see the value in breaking the age-old treaty with Amas, not when those animals so thoroughly bested us last time." She smiled. "But, alas, we came to this poor village on the very edge of Roldaer to perform our solemn duty, only to find our people slaughtered, and the sole survivor in cahoots with Amas."

Rage darkened his vision. "Liar! You murdered them all!"

The soldier behind Danil pushed him back down.

She appeared unmoved. "Even now, King Liam is amassing forces until the banner of vengeance."

Danil clenched his teeth, aghast. They'd been so

horribly mistaken to believe Magus Brianna headed a coterie of rogue mages. "Why would King Liam do this?" he gasped out.

"That is hardly the concern of peasants." Her pale eyes shifted to full white. "Let us move to more pressing matters, shall we? Namely, the shifters you've bent over for."

Danil felt like he'd been slapped. One of the soldiers leered at him. "I didn't—" He closed his mouth. He wasn't ashamed, and wouldn't deny something even if it had never happened.

"No? Not even the dragon whose mark your bear?"

Danil resisted when a soldier grabbed his clenched fist and forced it open. The glyph shone brightly in the sunlight.

"Will he come for you, Danil?" she asked. "We know he is close."

He said nothing, praying that Sonnen was already in the tunnels.

Ronan toyed with the handle of his firewhip. "Perhaps he needs time to think on things, my lady," the mage said, his voice a low purr.

"My patience grows thin, Ronan."

"Indeed, Great Lady." He bowed deeply. "But young Danil needs encouragement to move past his upset over the deaths in his village."

Danil watched him, uneasy. Cruelty glittered in Ronan's eyes.

Magus Brianna made a frustrated sigh. "I need him functional, Ronan. As much as I enjoy your methods, they hardly leave behind useful flesh."

Ronan's lip curled, though he didn't disagree.

"What do you even want the lodestone for?" Danil asked. "Aren't you powerful enough?" He glanced at the orb atop her staff. It pulsed slowly like a dying heart. He shuddered.

"The staff is but a bridge to controlling Kaul's lodestone," Brianna said, her eyes dreamy.

Danil frowned. "The lodestone can't be controlled by anyone."

"Kaul did, and he drank deeply," Brianna murmured. She stroked the orb. The corruption on her neck darkened. "And now, so shall I."

"I won't help you," he swore.

Brianna raised an eyebrow. "I think you'll find yourself willing to do a great many things, Danil. With the right persuasion."

"You're wrong."

"We'll see. Lord Ronan, let us begin preparations." She threw Danil a cold look, like winter come early. "Use this time wisely, Danil. My patience only runs so deep."

She turned with a sweep of her cloak. Soldiers bowed as she strode along the road leading back to Farin, her staff thudding like a drum on the ground.

Ronan gazed down at Danil, a cruel smirk on his face. He indicated for the soldiers to let him up. "I do not share Magus Brianna's patience, nor her belief that you are useful to us. At the earliest opportunity, I will gut you and leave you in the pit for the carrion rats to find." He smirked. "I could even do it now."

Danil swallowed as the soldiers tightened their grip on his arms.

Ronan stepped close, raising the firewhip. He pressed the handle against Danil's cheek. Danil flinched, expecting the hiss and burn of the whip as it ate away his flesh.

"Uh, uh," Ronan tutted softly. "Not yet. But soon," he promised. His breath brushed over Danil's skin. "You will lead us to the entrance of Kaul Mage-kin. And you will witness the might of our Great Lady coming into being. After that, I will have you."

Gorge rose in Danil's throat as he fought to school his face blank.

Ronan must have read his fear. Smiling coldly, he nodded to the soldiers.

Before he could dig in his feet, Danil was suddenly bodily lifted into the air and carried. With a heave, the soldiers threw him down the side of the pit.

He plummeted uncontrollably before crashing down onto something fetid and damp. He scurried back with a yell when he realized it was a torso, made unrecognizable by bloat and rotting flesh. Danil rolled over and vomited noisily.

Soldiers laughed from their stations above.

Wiping a shaking hand over his mouth, Danil looked up to see Ronan smirk before he disappeared from sight.

24

Only a few hours passed before Magus Brianna and Ronan returned. But they didn't return alone.

To Danil's shock, Hafryn was dragged behind Ronan. The firewhip wrapped around his throat, his face red from the struggle. The wolf looked freshly beaten, bruises evident on his face and arms. His braid had been yanked loose, his tunic torn and scabbard empty.

Danil met Hafryn's eyes and saw them widen in dismay.

"Look what we found sneaking into the village like a sly dog," Ronan said. He grinned, yanking Hafryn towards the edge of the pit. The wolf staggered but stayed upright with an effort.

Danil took an unconscious step up the side of the pit. An arrow suddenly landed inches from his feet. A soldier drew another bolt and took aim. Danil reluctantly stepped back down, chest tightening.

"Of course, the animal says there are no others sniffing about, but they won't stay hidden for long," Ronan continued.

Danil slid his gaze across to Brianna, who watched the

exchange silently. A gleam of contentment showed in her whitened eyes. More corruption showed above her bodice.

"The animal hasn't been forthcoming on why he's here, but we can hazard a guess," Ronan said. "Do you know why, rat?"

"No," Danil croaked.

"I think you do," Ronan countered, his smile turning cruel. "The Great Lady recognized him in a heartbeat. You've spent a lot of time with this one, haven't you?"

Danil held his gaze stonily as a few of the soldiers hurled invectives down at him. He didn't care.

Hafryn's mouth became downturned.

"Perhaps we're wasting our time," Brianna said. She tilted her head, showing the delicate line of her neck. "We have no use for the shifter if our traitorous guide has no care for him."

With a grin, Ronan yanked back on the handle of the firewhip. The cord snapped taut around Hafryn's throat. Hafryn's eyes widened as he tried to claw the firewhip loose. The cord turned deep red. Hafryn's eyes bulged.

"Stop!" Danil shouted.

Brianna appeared unmoved. "Tighter, if you please, Lord Ronan."

Ronan kicked the back of Hafryn's knees before placing a foot in the center of his back. He slowly tightened the cord, eyes bright with relish.

"Stop, please!" Danil shouted. "I'll do anything!"

Brianna raised her hand. Ronan loosened the cord slightly, expression rippling with displeasure as Hafryn let out a sudden, wheezing cough. His fingers tried to loosen the firewhip a little more, his flesh hissing at the movement.

"Do you know where the entrance to the lodestone is?" Brianna asked, voice mild.

Danil took a shaky breath. "I—" He struggled to speak, unable betray those he'd come to care for. Not when he was now part of an Amasian House. He didn't understand why Hafryn was here. The wolf wasn't supposed to be anywhere near Farin. Had he gone against Sonnen's orders? It made no sense.

Hafryn shook his head, trying to speak with his eyes. "Danil—" he choked out.

The firewhip constricted his throat once more. Ronan grinned as he stretched it taut.

"I'll take you!" Danil cried. "I know the way. Just stop, *please!*"

Brianna smiled. At her nod, Ronan eased off on his strangulation. The firewhip uncoiled from Hafryn's neck with a snap.

Hafryn collapsed onto the ground, coughing wetly.

"There, you see?" Magus Brianna said. She smiled. Her eyes glowed with power. "I knew you would come around."

Danil bowed his head in defeat.

ANOTHER FIVE MAGI had arrived in Farin since Magus Brianna gained control of the staff and orb. They joined her and Ronan in the march across the deadlands, accompanied by thirty of her soldiers. Ronan called them the personal guard of the Great Lady. It turned Danil's stomach.

With the afternoon sun already behind the mountains, long shadows cast a pall over the deadlands. At least Hafryn was by his side, wrists bound by simple rope. The cut on his throat looked painful, but the wolf walked with equanimity.

Danil let memory of the map guide him across the craggy rocks and exposed mineshafts. But as the escarpment drew inexorably closer, the desire to turn in a new direction took hold. A few of the soldiers faltered, but a dark look and crack of the firewhip kept them in check.

Dusk painted the clouds a dull pink by the time Danil stepped down into the shale field opposite the tunnel entrance. He gazed about, hoping to see shifters burst out of the sky. Only the quiet moan of a breeze sweeping across the stone met them. He paused, glancing at Hafryn.

The wolf studied the horizon, his expression carefully blank.

"We're close," Magus Brianna said. "I can feel the lodestone's power."

She stalked ahead. The shale barely stirred under her feet as she strode to the end of the field. To Danil's surprise, she passed the darkened mouth of the tunnel as if it were invisible. He shared a curious frown with Hafryn.

Hafryn snorted. "To its very core, the lodestone rejects her."

The mage whirled about, eyes flaring.

A soldier stepped up and struck Hafryn across the face. His head snapped to the side.

Danil jumped in front of the soldier and bared his teeth. "Hit him again and you'll get nothing more from me."

Sneering, the soldier looked ready to strike them both.

"Leave it, lieutenant," Brianna said, walking back to them. She took hold of Danil's arm. The grip burned. "Come. Show me."

Danil could feel the corruption skitter across his skin. He pulled loose. "Release the shifter and I'll do as you ask."

Her eyes flared.

"You can't find it without me." He held her gaze, unflinching.

A flash of annoyance crossed her face. "Help me reach

the lodestone and both you and the animal may go. I'll even give you a day's head start."

Danil narrowed his eyes. "Not much of an offer, considering your bent for spying on me."

Brianna smiled. "You would have made a satisfying apprentice. You still might."

Danil stared at her in revulsion.

A pair of soldiers lit torches and joined them at the mouth of the mineshaft. The air felt strangely energized. Brianna breathed in greedily. The orb seemed to glow in the firelight.

Danil gazed back the ruined landscape. It was bare of movement. Perhaps Sonnen had been unknowingly driven off by the magic that even now compelled Danil to back away from the dark entrance. Hafryn similarly studied the escarpment, though his expression was thoughtful. Ronan crowded in close. He thumbed the handle of his firewhip while glaring at the shifter.

"Lead on," Brianna said to Danil.

Danil grabbed a torch and stepped down. The first few feet were loose gravel and puddles made from snow runoff. The walls and ceiling gleamed in the torchlight like polished stone.

The magi, Hafryn and soldiers filed in after him. Their footsteps echoed loudly as he led them down to the first offshoot in the tunnel. Large sections had collapsed, forcing them to crawl in areas where the rocks were too large for the soldiers to move aside. Danil couldn't imagine Sonnen making his way through without having to do the same.

Danil edged around a mineshaft cut into the floor, his hands spread wide along the wall as he shuffled past. Torchlight didn't reach the bottom of the shaft.

A few of the soldiers balked at crossing. Towards the rear of the group, four soldiers edged back toward the exit.

"Enough!" Magus Brianna said. She swept her hand out, and suddenly the soldiers stiffened. Their faces held a familiar woodenness as they stood to attention. "Come."

The soldiers trudged past the inky void, unfettered by concern for their own wellbeing.

Hafryn's lip curled in distaste before Ronan shoved him into moving once more.

Danil took them further down, sweating in the strangely energized air. In some parts of the tunnel, the compulsion to leave felt overwhelming. He tried to recall the path he'd taken so long ago while in search of his mother. The memories seemed lost in a haze of desperation, and Danil found himself focusing instead on the thought of Hafryn, unfettered and wild in his wolf form, tongue lolling and tail in the air like a streamer. He yearned for him to enjoy such freedom again.

His feet led him down into a new side tunnel. Strange whisperings echoed off the walls, but a glance at the trailing magi showed that they seemed not to hear. Not even Magus Brianna, whose corruption had spread now to her jaw and left cheek. Sparks of white light danced off her fingers, frosting the walls.

The whisperings increased.

Danil trod over a slight dip in the floor, eyes on a darkened section of wall that indicated another side tunnel. A sensation tugged at him to stop.

He paused, suddenly nervous. "It's here."

Brianna motioned to one of the silent magi, who produced a small pouch. Inside, fine dust glittered in the torchlight. She licked her finger and dipped into the dust before sweeping her hand across the wall opposite them. The black stone seemed to melt away.

The hairs on Danil's arms rose. From the stone emerged a jagged-edged glyph he'd once seen on the spine of Kaul's journal.

Brianna gave a hum of pleasure.

"It appears you've led us true, rat," Ronan said with a mocking smile.

Magus Brianna swept her hand again, and the wall melted further away to reveal a staircase that clung to the side of an incredible chasm. A roaring sound pulled Danil's gaze to a waterfall that crashed down into the darkness far below. The echo of rushing water filled the chasm with a dull boom.

"Merciful gods," Hafryn breathed behind him.

"Behold, Kaul's legacy," Magus Brianna said triumphantly.

The hairs on Danil's arms rose as the whisperings struggled to be heard over the roar of the waterfall. There was something down there in the darkness. Something powerful.

Gods, where was Sonnen?

Brianna began her descent, her cloak splayed wide about her.

Ronan gave Danil a shove. "Move."

He did, dread lodged in his throat. The air felt thick with damp, the wet black rock sleek and gleaming in the torchlight.

A full hour passed as they made their way inexorably downwards. The damp settled into his clothing. Trailing behind him, with Ronan and three soldiers blocking him from reach, followed Hafryn. His red braid was bedewed, mist clinging to his dark eyelashes. He met Danil's gaze and nodded slightly.

The winding staircase came to an end on a wide platform of polished floor, though the waterfall continued to drop further down into the chasm. Brianna lifted her hand, releasing a series of magelights that spread out along the floor and then rose high, suddenly revealing a temple.

Danil stared in awe at the stark whiteness of the temple walls when everything surrounding it was black or slimed with moss and fungi. Warrior statues towered overhead, with crumbled swords and faces worn blank by time. Danil could tell they'd once stood tall, arms crossed and etched faces filled with foreboding.

He had no idea such a temple could exist below the deadlands.

Ahead, emerging from the white wall was a massive horse lying supine, legs flailed in the air as a warrior stood over it and drove a sword through its heart. Unlike all the other statues, this one was pristine, mane whipped back, the man's nostrils flared, his chest broad and powerful. Flecks of quartz and marble reflected in the magelight. Directly below the warrior, a pillared entrance led to a dark cavern beyond. Even from this distance, Danil could smell mossy loam and sun-sweetened water emanating from the cavern.

He looked uneasily at the slain horse once more.

"Kaul was horse-kin," Hafryn murmured, having come up beside him. His eyes were upraised, studying the statue with dislike. "A windrunner of the plains. He hated that aspect of himself, of course, and refused to shift. Naturally the pompous turd would make a monument of himself while denying half of what he was."

Ronan shoved Hafryn hard. "Quit your blathering," he ordered.

Hafryn's mouth thinned, eyes promising death. But he and Danil trailed after Magus Brianna, who strode across the platform.

To Danil's surprise, Hafryn caught his hand and intertwined their fingers together as they walked. The glyph on his palm grew warm.

Green eyes met his. He squeezed the wolf's hand and continued toward the white temple.

25

Beyond the pillars was a sprawling, unnaturally smooth cavern. A pearlescent gleam lay about the place, yet what immediately caught Danil's gaze was a well in the center of the cavern. It was small, no wider than a few feet, and yet the water within glowed so brightly it shone upon the ceiling high above. Danil felt a strange sort of peace as he looked upon it.

Beside him, Hafryn faltered a step. His face paled.

"What is it?" Danil asked under his breath.

"I-I thought it would be a crystal," Hafryn murmured, green eyes wide. "One that would be tainted by Kaul's workings." He shook his head, taking slow steps on the polished floor. "But it looks like the leylines have cleansed this place."

"That's a good thing, right?"

"Not if she gets near the well. The power of the leylines must have escaped from Kaul's workings. So now it collects like water in a cup. The Corrupt One will squat over it like a toad, and poison the leylines all the way to Amas." Hafryn looked ready to shift into wolf form and attack the mage.

A few feet ahead, Magus Brianna strode for the well. A ring of blackness spread out from underneath the staff every time she set it against the floor. The blood orb took on a new nimbus, casting the cavern in red.

Magus Brianna seemed to suddenly remember them. She turned about to incline her head at Ronan. "We are done with these two," she said.

Ronan grinned, firewhip stirring.

Without thought, Danil rolled before the firewhip bit his flesh. Hafryn unleashed a roar and tackled the mage. The air shimmered but strangely Hafryn didn't transform, and so human teeth bit down on Ronan's upraised arm. The mage bellowed in outrage.

A wooden-faced soldier came up behind Hafryn, sword raised. Danil rammed his shoulder into the soldier's guts and propelled him away. The hilt of the sword crashed down on his back. Danil hit the floor hard. He fought off another soldier, hearing Hafryn's desperate fight a few feet away.

Magus Brianna reached the well and lowered the blood orb into the water.

"No!" Hafryn cried out.

The orb struck hard stone.

"What—" Magus Brianna began, pulling the orb back.

The well abruptly blurred out of sight. In its place was a large swirling glyph etched deep into the stone floor. The mage stood in the center. Smaller glyphs spread out under the feet of the soldiers and magi.

Magus Brianna spun about, her cloak whirling. Her eyes widened in alarm.

The well shimmered into place about fifty feet deeper into the cavern. A sense of rightness swept over Danil. It was the true well.

Magus Brianna made to approach but struck up against an invisible wall.

A heartbeat later, the air between her and the well wavered, and suddenly there was Sonnen. At the dragon's side stood Blutark and Elania, along with more than thirty other Amasians. Danil even recognized the blue dragon among them. Sonnen's expression was severe.

Magus Brianna took an involuntary step back.

"You are bound, Corrupt One," Sonnen rumbled. "By fire and earth, you are bound."

The dragon raised his hand, and suddenly Danil could see a gossamer-thin net of silvery light over Brianna, the other magi and the soldiers. Sonnen muttered a word, and the five magi behind Ronan shrieked and screamed, thrashing in place before they collapsed to the ground.

A few of the soldiers seemed to awaken from their wooden-like slumber. They stared confusedly about the cavern and at the thrashing magi at their feet, and then backed away a few steps. A handful bolted for the pillars but were met by shifters.

Magus Ronan fared little better as the silvery net tightened over him. He stiffened like a board before falling to his knees and retching. Hafryn kicked away the firewhip and stood over the mage, looking ready to gut him.

Brianna appeared far more sanguine. With a smirk, she raised the staff and pressed the orb against the net. It disintegrated in a heartbeat. She stepped free.

Sonnen strode to meet her. Fire leapt from his hands and up his arms. Brianna shouted an unintelligible word, bloodied frost spewing from the orb. Sonnen met the attack, and the cavern reverberated with the crack of two elements colliding.

Brianna spun and pointed the orb at the remaining nets.

Ice poured over the magi and soldiers. The sound of glass shattering rang out as the nets collapsed.

Magus Ronan rolled to his feet with a roar of triumph. His hand snapped out, and the firewhip leapt into his grip.

Snarling, Hafryn raised his sword and knocked away the first biting attack of the firewhip.

Fighting broke out across the cavern as Amasians and Roldaerian soldiers clashed. Elania and Blutark stood over the incapacitated magi. Their hands moved rapidly as they wove a glyph above each mage.

Then Magus Brianna gouged the staff against the ground, and the orb darkened like rotten blood. The stench of putrefaction flooded the cavern.

One of the shifters closest to Danil cried out as a sickly white mark showed on her arm. The soldier she fought abruptly staggered and collapsed mid-strike. He coughed up plumes of frost.

Danil watched in horror as the soldier grew still.

Magus Brianna smiled.

"She's killing her own!" Hafryn cried.

"Pestilence and ice!" Sonnen roared. "Get back!"

It spread quickly, taking Amasian and Roldaerian alike. Cries rang out as fighters crumpled to the floor. The ice-rimed pestilence mottled the skin, eating away flesh.

Magus Brianna's smile widened as screams and cries rang out.

Danil gazed down at his arms, startled to see them bare of the consuming ice. He could only surmise it had something to do with his connection to the magus, whose curse still lay over him.

A short distance away, Hafryn gave a soft gasp and fell to one knee.

With a smirk, Ronan kicked him in the side. Hafryn

collapsed with a pained grunt. White ice showed along his arms.

The mage stood over him and swayed the tip of the firewhip above Hafryn's face. "Beg for me, dog."

Picking up a fallen sword, Danil roared as he swung at the firewhip.

It slithered to the side of its own volition.

Magus Ronan turned, blue eyes glittering. "Well, well. Haven't you grown brave." He stepped over Hafryn.

The wolf grabbed onto the mage's breeches but Ronan kicked him away.

Danil took a step back, feeling a mix of relief and terror as the mage followed.

The firewhip snaked across the floor.

"I used this on the people of Farin," Ronan taunted, giving the firewhip a flick. It hissed. "How they screamed and begged."

Danil raised his sword. Behind him, he could hear the crackle and spit of fire and ice clashing. Sonnen, at least, seemed able to defy Magus Brianna's spreading pestilence. The raging fire warmed across the nape of Danil's neck.

Ronan flicked the handle of the firewhip. It snapped out.

Danil barely had time to block the forked tongue from striking his eye. He glowered at the mage as he tightened his grip on the blade.

"My friend here has already tasted your flesh, rat," Ronan said. "Oh, but how it hungers for more."

Danil stepped back again, all too aware of the battle raging behind him between Sonnen and Magus Brianna.

"You were promised to me, rat. I have been so very, very patient."

The firewhip cracked upwards, hitting the sword with a loud clang. Danil flinched back, then quickly parried another biting blow. Ronan grinned, then sent the firewhip slithering along the floor before it flicked up and sank its forked tips into Danil's knee.

He staggered with a yelp. The firewhip bit him again before he managed a lucky strike.

Ronan laughed, then uttered a strange word. The firewhip brightened to red and lashed out, knocking the sword from Danil's grip.

He backed up, hands spread wide.

"Kneel, rat."

Danil's lips curled. "No."

Ronan grinned and unleashed the firewhip with a flick.

On instinct, Danil caught the coiling magic with both hands. It wrapped around his hands and wrists and squeezed. He instinctively gripped tight as fire burned across his skin. The glyphs on both palms brightened, spilling golden light between his fingers.

For a moment, Danil smelt wild loam and spring rain. His grip intensified.

An urgent whispering filled his mind.

'*Tighter,*' it belled.

Danil convulsively clenched his fists. The firewhip sizzled against the House glyphs. Blood welled over. For a heartbeat, the firewhip flickered white before returning to red.

Ronan frowned.

'*Again.*'

Against his better judgement, Danil obeyed. The firewhip whitened around his fists.

Ronan's eyes narrowed. "What are you doing?"

A rushing sound filled his ears as Danil concentrated on the golden light spilling between his hands. Flecks buzzed about the edges. He reached out and called on them. They latched onto the firewhip.

"Stop what you're doing," Ronan ordered, pulling back on the firewhip.

'Now.'

"Now!" Danil yelled. The golden light bit deep, engulfing the firewhip. The red sputtered out, and then a strange whirring sound filled the air.

Ronan released the handle, eyes widening.

A heartbeat later, the firewhip shattered in Danil's hands. Splinters of cord, sharpened like glass, blew over Ronan in a backlash of power that sent the mage catapulting across the cavern. He struck the far wall with a bone-crunching snap.

"*No!*"

Danil whirled to see Magus Brianna barreling toward him, fingers claw-like. Her face was a rictus of fury.

A wall of flame suddenly blocked her path.

She spun back to Sonnen. The dragon was on his feet, his skin splotched with ice. But his eyes remained fiercely aflame. Fire arced up his arms.

"We are not done," the dragon vowed as he straightened.

Brianna raised the staff. The ice pestilence rocked Sonnen back on his feet.

Danil picked up a fallen sword, skirting wide.

Magus Brianna tracked his movements with a small smile. "Stupid little guide. I'll leave you to last so that you may enjoy the new world I have wrought. We will bathe in dragon blood together."

With a guttural roar, Sonnen snapped fire at her. Brianna brushed it aside with a sweep of the blood orb.

Gripping the hilt tight in both hands, Danil waited for

her attention to focus fully on Sonnen. She skirted out of easy reach.

Then he felt something tug at him. The quiet whisperings he'd heard in the cavern and beyond returned. Danil vigorously shook his head to clear it.

'Join us,' it rang.

Danil's eyes turned to the well. The tug grew stronger, like a physical yearning. The scent of wildness and freshly turned soil filled the cavern.

'*Come.'* The word was like a clarion in his bones.

He dropped the sword. The roar of fire smashing up against pestilence hissed out behind him.

Danil cautiously climbed the three steps and looked down into the well. The glowing water was a startling, cooling blue that beckoned him.

'*Come,'* it repeated.

With a slow breath, Danil lowered his hand into the water. Blood swirled and then dissipated into the depths. The House glyph on his palm dropped flecks of gold into the bottom of the well.

The water stirred.

Something grabbed hold of Danil's wrist.

"*No!*" Brianna screamed.

With a gentle tug, it pulled him into the water.

26

They stride the cavern, seeking darkness.

They see it in thin lines of black ice that gorge upon an iridescent light barely still flickering with life.

"This one remains with us," they say, and brush their fingers across the blackness. The tendrils fall apart like gossamer. The iridescent one brightens, strengthens, and green eyes open with wonder.

They decide it is a pretty green.

There are more in need of aid, and so they sweep across the cavern until the blackness is no more.

Dozens of greyfolk lie supine while the black tendrils feast upon them.

"These are also ours."

They break apart the tendrils, and slowly, life returns.

Among the fallen are five greyfolk with a flickering of iridescence in their bellies.

"We are not yours," they say, and return the iridescence to themselves.

All that remains is the Corrupt One, spinning her web like a spider. At her side is a revenant of Darkness.

They remember a time before Darkness, when they had romped across the surface untrammeled by exploitation, the sun on their backs charging them with warmth. They remember tasting the triumph of spring, the first shoots unfurling from the seed, the gambol of life on fertile soil, the chittering in burrows and on branches.

"We have waited long enough."

They take the revenant from the Corrupt One, and dissolve the last remnant of the one who had so twisted them and left them in the cold and quiet.

The Corrupt One raises her hands and spews forth blackness, but her rage is like a pebble on a mountainside.

All that remains is the stolen iridescence roiling in her belly. They take that, too.

Then they return to the wellspring, where green purpose burbles once more.

27

D anil returned to awareness.

    He leaned over the water, his fingers skimming the surface. In his other hand sat a glass orb whose color ran clear like icicles in the winter sun. He stared at it, but felt no remnant of Kaul within.

A soft query sounded at the back of his mind.

With a nod, Danil lowered the orb into the water. Something swirled around to gently take it from his grasp.

"Impossible!" Magus Brianna shrieked.

She stood at the base of the steps, hair wild and clothes askew. Her eyes were no longer milky, returned instead to their previous pale blue. Her skin appeared similarly revived, no longer marked by corruption. At her feet lay the shattered remains of the bone staff, the blood orb gone.

Behind her, the cavern stirred to life. Amasians and Roldaerians soldiers alike rose to their feet, dazed. A few soldiers openly wept at having been so close to death. The five magi scurried to the pillars, only to be blocked by the nearby shifters. Only Ronan didn't stir, lying crumpled and unmoving against the far wall.

Hafryn padded toward the steps, green eyes filled with curiosity and wonder. "*Fala*?" he said, staring.

Sonnen strode up to Danil and took hold of his chin. He gazed deeply into Danil's eyes, and Danil wondered what he saw there.

"It is not impossible," the dragon said, releasing him. Sonnen turned to glower down at Brianna. "He is of Roldaerian blood but with the House of Corros on his palm. As once was Kaul before him, Danil is of both our kingdoms, mage."

She shook with fury. "The well is *mine!*"

Flames showed in Sonnen's eyes. "Perhaps you have not yet noticed, Corrupt One. By Danil's will, the well and its leylines are closed to you. All kiandrite is closed to you. And ever will it be!"

Brianna's face hardened with fury. She raised her hands, fingers claw-like as she snarled an unintelligible word. Nothing happened, and Brianna gaped at her hands in horror.

Sonnen took a single step down. "In your quest for power, you sought to become the anathema of our shared magicks. You thought, like Kaul before you, that a lodestone would bend to your will," he growled. "But the leylines have chosen a new custodian. One who will heal the damage wrought by your machinations." The dragon's voice rang out across the cavern like a proclamation.

A couple of shifters nodded in agreement.

"He means you, *fala*," Hafryn noted with a grin.

Danil looked at Sonnen in surprise.

The dragon ignored him, taking another step down toward the mage. She swallowed, then lifted her chin.

"But what to do with you, hmn?" the dragon rumbled. He studied her and then swept a flame-filled gaze to the five magi pressed up against the wall beside the pillars. They shuffled their feet nervously. "Indeed, you are worthy of death."

The leylines set to murmuring. Danil craned to hear.

"And yet, not here," Sonnen continued. His face revealed no hint that he'd heard the leylines. "This place has already been befouled by your malevolence. We will not taint its return to us by spilling blood." He smiled humorlessly, baring teeth. "I suggest you don't ever attempt to return to Amas. The well is rather angry with you, and its memory is long."

Brianna cast a nervous glance at the well. The glowing liquid stirred as if to slosh up against the sides.

"Danil, if you will," Sonnen murmured.

Startled, he stepped forward.

"Like so," the dragon said, weaving an intricate symbol into the air.

Danil followed suit. The ground below him swelled with power.

Brianna's eyes widened, seeming to recognize the glyph that took shape. "No!"

Danil completed the glyph. It held in the air before him, gleaming like gold, before sweeping across the cavern. It carried Brianna off her feet, so too the remaining magi and soldiers.

"So you are banished," Sonnen growled. "Banished for life and in memory." His voice boomed. "Be gone from this place. And good riddance."

The glyph expanded and brightened with ferocity, until Danil was forced to clench his eyes from being blinded. The air seemed to contract, then with the sound of a distant bell, the light extinguished.

Blinking rapidly, Danil looked about the cavern. A few shifters stood about, scrubbing their eyes.

Hafryn met his gaze and smiled.

Brianna, her magi and soldiers were gone.

28

They emerged from the tunnel after dawn. Danil stared about the deadlands, blinking at the brightness. He didn't think they'd been in the cavern for so long.

"Time moves differently in sacred spaces," Sonnen said.

Danil hadn't realized it was sacred, and said as much.

The lines about the dragon's eyes tightened. "It will be," he promised, having already charged two shifters with the unenviable task of carrying Ronan's body from the cavern. "Over the next few weeks, we'll remove the monuments Kaul made for himself. Though I expect with time the well itself will dissipate as the leylines find new routes across the land."

The leylines hummed in affirmation. Danil could sense them already seeking paths through crevices and tunnels and mineshafts.

Danil almost smiled. "Let's keep things comfortable in the meantime."

Sonnen rumbled in agreement.

The dragon sent a force ahead to Farin to ferret out any

last remaining Roldaerian magi and soldiers. The shifters returned hours later with news that the village sat abandoned, with signs of a hasty retreat.

With a respectful nod at Danil, the leader added that a few had remained behind to fill the pit and afford the slain villagers burial rites befitting honored folk.

Throat closing over, Danil thanked the leader.

Hafryn touched his elbow. "When you're ready to pay your respects, Danil, I'd like accompany you."

The leylines murmured their approval.

By lunchtime, Danil found himself under a makeshift awning in a wide deadland gully as tents and cooking stations were erected all around him. Curious onlookers crowded around the awning as Elania tended to his smattering of scrapes and bruises. He did his best to ignore the curious looks, dismayed to be under the regard of so many.

"You're somewhat notorious now," Hafryn pointed out from where he perched on a stool, having had all his own wounds healed by the leylines when they shook off Magus Brianna's dark magic. Danil appeared to be the only one still sporting injuries from the encounter.

"To keep you grounded," Elania said with a dimpled grin.

Danil flinched as she swabbed a gash on his forearm. The snow leopard didn't even bother with her ever-present paintbrush to augment her ministrations.

The leylines thrummed underfoot and cheerily ignored his consternation.

Elania seemed to share their sentiments. "Just because you can wave your hand around and have leylines clamor to your will does not mean you get special treatment," she said, her amber eyes betraying her amusement. "Now, quit fidgeting!"

"The gentle treatments of a warrior-healer is an acquired taste, Danil," Blutark chortled.

Elania threw the bear a glare with such venom that Blutark transformed into his Trueform. He ducked behind a grinning Hafryn, breath chuffing in what could only be humor.

The surrounding shifters laughed.

It got Danil thinking, though. "Say, why didn't any of you shift in the cavern?" A raging dragon or two would have been rather helpful.

Sonnen leaned against a bench a few feet away, watching the proceedings with a faint smile. "Believe me, it wasn't to test your mettle," he said, to a round of chuckles. The dragon sobered and folded his arms. "As a halfbreed, Kaul hated every aspect that made him Amasian. In a temple he built in his own honor, it stands to reason that there would be magicks to deny all shifters the right to transform."

Danil sighed, shaking his head. "I had no idea there was a temple right under the deadlands. No one in Farin did."

"We might have taken a misstep there, too," Hafryn admitted with a wry grin. "Kaul's bent was to force kiandrite to his will. We assumed we would find a crystal made from power stolen from leylines."

"And that it could be spirited out of the temple long before the magi arrived," Blutark added.

Elania set down a damp cloth. "That's why we sent Hafryn to Farin to be captured."

Danil looked sharply at the wolf.

Hafryn shrugged self-deprecatingly. "We had quite the plan to trap the magi. You had to know it was safe to guide them into the tunnels." He gave Danil a fond look. "I know you, *fala*. You would have stayed stubborn to the end. And I was right. I'm only sorry I wasn't there earlier to ease your torment."

Danil ducked his head and tried not to think of the refuse pit. It would be in his nightmares for a long time. "Being a deadland scavenger saved my life," he murmured eventually. He glanced at Hafryn. "My people died the day you stole from me."

The wolf grimaced. "Well, I'm glad you were there to steal from," he said. "You always had the ability to find kiandrite, even when there should have been none to find."

"The leylines recognize their allies," Elania observed.

Danil raised an eyebrow at that. He sent out a questioning thought and received a gentle affirmation. But there'd been other situations where he'd barely survived being out in the deadlands, like the time he'd miraculously survived a cave-in, or when he'd wandered about sick with fever and had no memory of returning to Farin with a pouch of kiandrite. Surely the leylines had played no hand in them.

The leylines suddenly felt...smug.

Scrubbing his face, Danil decided this was all going to take some getting used to.

Sonnen sighed. "Allowing the magi into the temple was our mistake," he admitted. "We assumed we would find a lodestone of incredible power, not a sacred grove where the leylines had pooled together and then been left to languish. Regardless, I expected our trap in the temple to work."

Danil shook his head. "Magus Brianna knew, didn't she?"

"Though she appears to have had no greater knowledge of Kaul than us, she rightly guessed what was needed to gain control of a lodestone's power," Sonnen conceded. "In his arrogance, Kaul keyed the lodestone to work only for him—one had to be both Roldaerian and Amasian to access its power."

"That's why she went after Kaul's remnants to make the staff," Danil surmised.

Sonnen inclined his head in agreement.

Danil glanced down at his right palm, where the House of Corros glyph shone as if freshly painted. He traced the edge and felt a soft warmth when it brightened.

"Did you know?" he asked Sonnen, not able to look up. "When you gave me this?"

Sonnen reached across and placed a hand over the glyph. It fairly hummed at the reaffirmation. "The welcoming to my House is heartfelt, Danil of Farin. In truth, I thought it irrelevant to the task we faced." He sat back with a smile.

"But not so irrelevant now, right, dragon?" Hafryn asked, grinning.

The dragon released a huff.

Hafryn winked at Danil. "I believe Sonnen promised you a welcoming feast."

Danil glanced at the dragon.

Sonnen inclined his head. "I have indeed been remiss in my duty. And you are most welcome among us, Danil of Roldaer and Amas." He stood, clapping his hands. "Come. It's time you discovered how Amasians *truly* live."

29

It was a whirl of dancing, feasting and the trill of pipes that lasted long into the night. For the first time, Danil tried a tankard of honeymead, a hot sugar-spiced ale laced with ground-up kiandrite. It set his head to spinning, with the clamor of leyline voices ringing in his mind.

Hafryn steadied him with a laugh. "Honeymead's quick on the tongue but heavy in the blood, *fala*."

Danil leaned against Hafryn as he struggled to regain his balance. "I can hear the leylines!" he blurted out.

"Custodian!" someone nearby shouted.

A cheer rang about them.

Hafryn's green eyes sobered slightly. "Try not to drink too quickly," he said, before setting Danil off to dance with Elania and Blutark.

The snow leopard and bear weren't the only shifters to dance with him. Danil found himself deep amongst the throng, the music echoing about the gully. Patril, the commander of Altonas, proved particularly skilled, spinning Danil about for a number of songs until he was dizzy from laughter.

After a time, Danil begged off, in need of a place to cool down and gather his breath. He wandered up to the top of the gully, where the din of the celebration was muted by a breeze sweeping across the deadlands. The air carried the scent of fresh loam and grass underfoot, and Danil breathed deeply. Though the deadlands seemed quiescent, he could sense the stirring far below. Once the leylines reached the surface, the deadlands would be reimagined with ferocity.

Danil looked toward Farin, dark and quiet on the edges. Sorrow tugged at his heart. He'd never go back—not even when the village inevitably became inhabited once more by folk with no knowledge of what had transpired. Eyes stinging, he sent a silent farewell. It was time to look forward.

He watched the moonlight play upon the black rocks for a time before abruptly realizing he'd not seen Hafryn in quite a while. Turning about to search for him, Danil suddenly noticed a figure perched on a nearby boulder.

Sonnen.

The dragon sat with one boot propped upon the rock, elbow resting on his knee. Golden eyes shone in the moonlight.

Danil had no idea how long he'd been there, though he suspected he was the interloper. He sketched a hasty bow. "Beg pardon, Sonnen," he said, heading for the path that led back down into the gully.

"Stay, Danil," the dragon rumbled, voice mild. "You are quite welcome."

Hesitating, Danil trudged over and leaned against the rock at the dragon's side. It felt sun-warmed along his back.

"I, too, am in need of respite," Sonnen said with a half-smile. "And a moment's reflection on a day that very nearly ended in disaster."

Danil nodded. Facing death was something he'd never grow accustomed to. "In the cavern, you called me a custodian."

"I did," Sonnen said.

"How do you know for sure?"

Sonnen gave him a long study, his face half in shadow. "You saved the Roldaerian soldiers, did you not? And also the magi, undeserving as they were."

Danil nodded.

"You gave mercy because they are folk from your own kingdom."

Danil shifted, uncomfortable with the criticism.

Sonnen shook his head, the flames in his eyes gentle like a hearth-fire at the end of winter's day. "That is temperance. Forbearance." He straightened, staring out at the horizon. "Imbalance is what created the deadlands, Danil. Kaul strode the line between our two kingdoms, but he chose Roldaer. And so there was cataclysm. In his place, however, you chose both." He patted the ruined rock beneath him. "This place will flourish once more because of it."

In the back of Danil's mind, the leylines made a low murmur of agreement. They were already seeking the surface, stretching up through the crevices in the rock. Between his boots, a fragile shoot burst free of the gravel, a single leaf made silver in the moonlight.

Danil looked out over the jagged landscape. "If Brianna spoke true about King Liam, then we've not seen the end of this. I can sense the kiandrite in Roldaer and it's...waning. If the magi have the king's ear, he'll send an army to battle against Amas. They need the kiandrite."

"But there will be no battles here," Sonnen rumbled.

Danil glanced at him in curiosity.

"You'll see it in a few weeks," the dragon said with a

satisfied smile that bared teeth. "The deadlands are renewed. It will not allow itself to be used as anything but a sanctuary." Sonnen leaned back against the rock. "The Roldaerians will try, of course. And they will learn."

Danil watched as dawn slowly painted the clouds pink and gold. "I'm not sure allowing Brianna to live was a good idea," he admitted.

Sonnen released a deep sigh. "Stripped of her power, her death serves no purpose. As a warning to other magi of the downfalls of greed, however, she is a potent message." His mouth tilted humorlessly. "Of course, we will see in time if setting her loose was folly."

It was hardly comforting, but it had to be enough.

Danil settled back to watch the deadlands brighten into day, listening to the contented burble of the leylines as life began anew beneath their feet.

AT DAWN, Danil found the wolf in one of the many tents splayed about the gully. The tent was much smaller than the one they'd shared in the borderlands, and sparsely furnished with a pair of sleeping pallets and a small chest with a basin atop for rudimentary washing. A lamp hung from a nail in the center pole, sputtered out as the sun cast a soft orange glow against the canvas wall.

"So here's where you've been hiding," Danil said, folding his arms.

Hafryn washed his hands and elbows, avoiding his gaze. "Cleaning up after a long night is hardly hiding, *fala*."

"There's feasting still going on outside. I didn't see you for most of the night," he pointed out. "I would have liked to share the celebrations with you."

Hafryn scrubbed the back of his neck. "It wasn't my intent to disappoint you. I had much to think about."

"Such as?"

The wolf frowned at him. Clearly, he didn't enjoy being pressed. "Very well." The wolf huffed out a breath. "The deadlands hasn't had a custodian in centuries, and let's face it, the last one wasn't anything to emulate."

Danil nodded, waiting.

"This place has certain quirks. By becoming the new custodian, you are bound here for all your life."

Danil stoppered his heart. "Oh. I didn't know that," he said softly. "Elania and Blutark have already offered to stay on," he added, recalling drunken proclamations earlier in the night.

"I'm glad. There are no better folk to have at your back than those two."

"What about you?" Danil asked. "Will you stay as well?"

"I'd be more than happy to help."

"Help," Danil said, tasting the word.

"Yes."

Danil studied Hafryn, unused to the wolf's evasiveness. He was normally so upfront.

The leylines clamored in his mind with thoughts and suggestions. With dawning understanding, Danil realized they'd purposefully guided him to this place. Hafryn had been the first Amasian he'd spoken to, the first he'd fought with and the first he'd turned to. He recalled the soft murmurings of the wind between the crevasses when he'd first fled Magus Brianna all those weeks ago. Even so deep underground, the leylines had inexorably led him to this wolf.

Danil made a frustrated sound. He felt raw and

uncertain, although the path was laid out before him if he dared take it.

"*Fala*?"

"Are custodians celibate?" he asked, then felt immediately foolish for speaking.

Hafryn started. "I—no. Not to my knowledge."

Danil forced his spine to straighten. He looked the wolf dead in the eye. "Well, then."

The wolf tilted his head. Realization slowly dawned in his green eyes. "I think I may have had too much honeymead..."

Danil bit back a smile. "You're an idiot, wolf."

Hafryn looked mildly affronted, but amusement showed in his eyes. "Be kind, *fala*. My soul has been resigned to hounding you across the deadlands for all time."

Danil rolled his eyes, unable to stop his grin. "You needn't chase me anymore, wolf," he said.

Hafryn took a step closer. "Are you certain? Who else will I steal from?" he murmured, green eyes bright.

"I'm sure you'll find someone," Danil said dryly.

"Unlikely."

With a quelling breath, Danil took hold of the wolf's hand. He smiled. "I'd give you everything, anyway."

Hafryn's eyes widened in wonder.

A warm peace settled over him as he met Hafryn's gaze. "Here, let me show you."

With a gentle tug, Danil led him to their pallet.

30

A few weeks later, Danil squatted beside a stream and sank his hands into the cool, crisp water. Sunshine beat down on his back and bare arms as he straightened. At the shadowed base of a boulder, the first tree fern stretched out its fronds. The stream itself ran thick with salmon.

Danil raised a hand to cut down the glare as he looked across the deadlands. Deep lines of verdant green cut across the black. In the distance, Farin no longer sat empty. Vines and trees sprouted from the land in wild abandon.

"You're not going to catch dinner like that," Hafryn said as he tossed his line back into the stream. He gnashed his teeth at the school of fish that idled past.

"You're doing a fine job without me," Danil said, bumping shoulders as he came to sit beside the wolf.

A shadow in the form of a great dragon passed over them, fresh from Corros and the shifter army amassing there. The dragon wheeled above them, shining golden, before heading for the camp set up just a mile south.

"Great. Now we *definitely* won't catch anything," Hafryn muttered as fish scattered.

Danil lay back and idly listened as the leylines sang of voles and hares and birdfolk making homes amidst the new underbrush. A short span from Farin, a cacophony of wildflowers enveloped where the refuse pit once sat.

He avoided the place.

"You'll have to go someday, *fala*," Hafryn told him one evening as they lay together in the quiet of the camp.

Someday, he thought. But not yet. Perhaps when there was peace, when the threat of Roldaer's king and his magi had passed.

In the meantime, he would guard this place. With the help of Elania and Blutark and even Sonnen, he'd learn to strengthen and protect the leylines already dancing along the surface. With Hafryn at his side and an army at his back, he'd meet every threat with a resounding war cry.

Closing his eyes, he released his mind and wandered along the leylines as they spread out far into the land. He sought out the flecks and veins of kiandrite, the nuggets stored in jars within magi workrooms and boltholes. He found the enclave below the Magi Council, and sensed the kiandrite ingested by mages throughout Roldaer.

Without hesitation, he released a promise. It belled within every speck of kiandrite, resonating like a clarion all the way to the halls of the Roldaerian king.

Amas will never be taken.

A mage looked about her workroom, eyes wide.

The slaughter of your own people will not go unanswered.

Perched upon a decorative throne, a grey-haired man clenched his fist.

If you plan to attack, you will lose.

In a training salle, a military commander stumbled mid-strike.

Danil felt the leylines coalesce around him, charging him with power. He released a final message, feeling the weight of an entire shifter kingdom behind it.

We are ready.

ABOUT THE AUTHOR

K K NESS is the pen name of identical twins living in Australia. They both share a love of characters whose antics make them happy, and enjoy competing against each other to see how much mayhem can happen in a book. They currently reside in sunny Queensland with various family and animal friends.

Visit their website for the latest releases and updates.

www.kkness.com

Before you leave...
Reviews are the lifeblood of authors. If you enjoyed Messenger (or even if you didn't), please leave a review on the way out. Your support and feedback is everything!